Into the Rabbit Hole

The Hidden Archives

In scientia fidei robur

Nisi qui habet scientiam in fide

Book 5

Books by Micah T. Dank

Into the Rabbit Hole *series*

Book 1: Beneath the Veil

Book 2: The Sacred Stones

Book 3: The Secret Weapon

Book 4: Pangaeas Pandemic

Book 5: The Hidden Archives

Coming Soon!

Book 6: The Final Type

Into the Rabbit Hole

The Hidden Archives

Book 5

Micah T. Dank

SPEAKING VOLUMES, LLC
NAPLES, FLORIDA
2021

The Hidden Archives

ISBN 978-1-64540-462-0

To my agent Nancy that took a chance on me, to my Publishing House Speaking Volumes that took an even greater chance. To Michelle my publicist and to Mark Steeves who has been so helpful throughout this all. Finally to the Twitter Podcast community that has opened its arms open wide to me, I thank you all from the bottom of my heart.

A lot of our beliefs came from our parents; the good and the bad. Don't blame them, a lot of their beliefs came from their parents, don't blame them either. You see, this is conditioning. It's like a cycle. We can have a strong opinion about something that we've never experienced. We can view something a certain way simply because our great-grandfather did, and no one broke the cycle. We are moving into a time where we are no longer adopting beliefs; we are thinking for ourselves—Mark Sutton

Chapter One

I am profusely sweating at this point. Sweat has started to drip into my eyes and I can't see anymore. I should have brought an ice cube to suck on to keep this from happening. Slowly, my breathing started to get more shallow as I began to focus on the task in hand. This has happened so many times before, but for some reason this time, my entire body felt like it was shutting down. I tried to open my eyes, but the sting from the sweat was too much to bear, so I kept them shut and just hoped that I knew what I was doing at this point. All my friends were 3000 miles away from me at this point and I was all alone. Then, all at once, my body began tingling from

Micah T. Dank

my toes up my spine. Pretty soon, I was shuddering, and out of nowhere, it felt like a giant bolt of lightning hit me. My arms gave out and I collapsed in a pile of human flesh. My mind was void of any thoughts as I concentrated on my breathing and returning my heart rate to normal. I was completely numb and lay there for a few minutes. Then, when I was about to pass out, I heard a voice.

Your experiences have brought you to this level of perception. Your struggles have not been in vain, as they have given you wisdom of divine understanding. Do not seek approval from a lower level of awareness, as you will only become disenchanted by the futility in trying to conform to a place you have outgrown. Perceive what is within your elevated frequency of awareness and you will continue to rise to new heights of wisdom and understanding—Anonymous

Chapter Two

"Orgasm is the closest we get to God until we die. Ecstasy is the nature of Existence. There is a Universe for the simple reason that it is ecstatic," Hannah said.

"It was incredible, as usual," I replied.

"Alan Watts," she said.

"I figured as much," I replied.

I rolled over and sat up ass naked and picked up the pack of cigarettes from the lampstand. I shook it, you know, to wake the cancer up, and pulled one out and lit it.

"Babe, do me a favor. Hand me two Tylenol out of my purse, will you?" she asked.

"Aw, I'm sorry sweetie," I started smirking, "are you sore?" I asked.

"Relax killer, you didn't murder anyone, I just have a headache that's all," she said.

"If that's the case, then why are your dinner-plate sized nipples still so hard right now?" I asked as I tossed her the bottle and a bottle of water.

"Shut up fuck boy," she laughed.

"It's because you're half Italian isn't it?" I asked.

"Ew, ass," she said as she threw the pill bottle at my head. I caught it and stood up and walked to the bathroom to take the post coital piss.

"Can you at least shut the door while you do that?" she asked.

"Sorry no can do, hands are full right now," I said.

I heard my cell phone starting to ring.

"Hey baby it's for you," Hannah said.

"Who is it?" I asked.

"Not sure, but it's a California area code. Did you give any girl your number while you're out here on our honeymoon?" Hannah asked.

"What? No, of course not," I said as I walked back into the bedroom.

"Well, too bad. We could have had some fun," she smiled and threw me the phone.

"Don't tease me woman, and definitely don't let Larisa hear that you said that," I said as I answered the phone.

"Hello? Yes, this is him. How did you get my number? Wait, can you just repeat that again slowly for me? I see. When? Well, it just so happens I'm on my long-deserved honeymoon and I'm still in Cali. Yeah. E-mail me all the information and we'll be there tomorrow. No, thank you for the call. Seriously. I look forward to meeting you tomorrow," I said as I hung up.

"Who was that, baby?" Hannah asked.

I sat down on the bed and snubbed out my cigarette and lit up another one. I always chain smoke during adrenaline rushes.

"If I told you, you wouldn't even believe me," I said.

"Come on Graham, who was it?" Hannah asked.

"Tell you what. Google the number on your phone and tell me what you get back," I said as I gave her the number.

She fidgeted around with the phone for a minute while I stared at her perfect C breasts just resting on her chest. I was going to be ready to go again. I am in Cali, so maybe I'll go get a wetsuit before I try this again. 100-degree weather is insane. Finally, I saw her eyes widen, then she shook her head and put her phone down.

"So, it was a wrong number wasn't it?" she asked.

5

"What did you find?" I asked.

"It was Venus Lair Studios. What the hell did they want from you? Did they find your headshot from when you were a real fuck boy?" she asked.

"Hannah, they want to meet me tomorrow and talk about making my book series into a movie series," I said.

You could hear her blood circulating in the room that's how quiet it was for about two minutes until she spoke up. Love Hannah, but typical fashion, she's the type to bring up concerns first.

"Babe, that's amazing, but our lives have already been so crazy so far. And your books, I mean what we've been through is so controversial, what if people come after us?" she said.

"People already have come after us, we're still here, though aren't we?" I asked.

"I just worry, if they make a series out of this, it's going to anger a LOT of people," she said.

"I know. But let's just go there and see what they have to say," I said.

"Alright. Where are they located?" she asked.

"Getting instructions emailed to me. Probably down-town LA," I said.

"I'm really proud of you, but if you think you don't have privacy now, if you go through with this, you'll be trapped. Remember, you can become infamous, but you can never become unfamous," she said.

"Very true baby. I just feel like it's my life's calling to get these stories out to as many people as possible. Maybe then they would be able to move beyond religion, and we can evolve to a higher level in Aquarius," I said.

"You've been listening to Eckhart Tolle again haven't you?" she said.

"Shut up. Oh great, just got the email," I said as I scanned the information presented to me.

"I have to call Rick," I said.

She nodded.

Rick's brother and my father were great friends in College. Rick was my lawyer, but not lawyer. He always helped out with what I wanted to do as far as publishing and how to go about it. I called him. I was hoping he could fly cross country today for a meeting tomorrow. He picked up on the fourth ring. I explained to him everything that was going on and he said it would be his pleasure to mediate the meeting tomorrow. We hung up, and I gave him the address of our hotel. Then I remembered that we were still in San Diego. That orgasm had me shook. I told him we'd meet on Sunset tomorrow around noon, the meeting was going to be at 3. I hung up the phone and turned to my wife.

"Well babe, as much as it pains me to say it, get up and put some clothes on, we have to go," I said.

"Where are we going?" she asked.

"Going clothes shopping for tomorrow," I said.

"You're such a girl sometimes," she said as she rolled her eyes back at me so hard it would give the wrestling Undertaker a hard on.

"Love you too babe," I said.

"Hey sweetie?" she asked.

"What's up?" I asked.

"What do you think about the Library of Alexandria thing? Do you think it still exists?" she asked.

"If it did, if hypothetically it still existed somewhere, it would contain the most precious writings the world has ever known. Only 1% of ancient writings have ever been uncovered. Nowadays anyone on the internet can become famous forever. It's a catalogue of nonsense. But let's forget about that for now, let's go out for a little joyride right now," I said.

"Good, because I could use a coffee right about now," she said.

"You do know that caffeine doesn't actually give you energy, it just blocks the adenosine receptors in your brain, the receptors that let you know when you are tired," I said.

"Thanks for the mansplaining," she replied.

"I'd rather be hated for who I am, than loved for who I am not," I said.

"Mr. Rogers?" she asked.

"No, Kurt Cobain," I said.

We packed up our things and got dressed. We got into our rental and started driving around looking for clothing stores. LA was too expensive, and I was really enjoying sweating to death right now. I didn't know it at the time, but my life would both change for the better and worse.

Chapter Three

We met at noon. I gave Rick a hug and introduced him to Hannah. He smiled. We sat down and had lunch at a bistro, and he went over some points with me. Technically he wasn't my lawyer, but he offered to act on my behalf. He does contracts for a living and damn sure knew his stuff.

After lunch we made our way to Venus Lair Studios. I showed them my ID and they let us right in. We parked the car and one of the people came outside to meet us.

"Hi, my name is Dexter. You must be Graham Newsdon," he said to Rick.

"Actually no, I'm his attorney," Rick said.

"Wait, so you're Graham Newsdon?" he asked.

"I am," I said.

"But you're so young. How do you know half the things you wrote about in your books?" he asked.

"I've had motivation. Let's just leave it at that. Can we go inside, it's too hot for life out here," I said.

"Right, absolutely. Follow me," Dexter said.

He led us into the building and into an elevator. We went to the top floor, the penthouse naturally. Inside there was one other man sitting.

"Welcome Graham, I see you've brought your kids," the man said to Rick.

"What is it with you guys?" I asked.

"Sorry. Our apologies. Truly, very sorry. This is Graham," Dexter said as he pointed at me.

The other man's eyes got wide and then he composed himself. I saw that threw him off guard.

"Of course you are. Forgive the rudeness. Can I get you guys something to drink? Sparkling water, juice, vodka maybe?" the man asked.

I was tempted.

"No but if you guys have any magic mushrooms, I'll take some," I said.

Rick shot me a mortified look.

"Are you serious?" Dexter asked.

"Only mildly. I'm sorry, it's been a rough day. Can we sit?" I asked.

"Of course. Please, this is my boss John, but everybody calls him Goomba.

"Goomba, really?" I asked.

"Yes, Goomba," John said.

"That's an amazing name," I said.

"Thank you, Graham. Now let's get started. We've been keeping an eye on you. Your Aquastream videos have a ton of followers and your books are doing quite well. I don't have the exact numbers, but I'll tell you they had such an interesting take. Did you really go through everything you went through in those books?" Goomba asked.

"I did. Well, we did," I said as I turned to my wife.

"And you must be Hannah. I recognize you from the books," Dexter said.

"Oh really? You've both read the books? I asked.

"You have something special with them kid. I don't know anybody that puts thoughts like you do. Also, your friends are brilliant. The way you work as a team to solve mysteries. It's like Scooby Doo meets McGuyver meets the Power Rangers," Goomba said.

"Well, thank you," I said.

"What are you offering?" Rick asked.

"Right down to business, I like this guy. Well first, we want the exclusive rights and all media," Dexter said.

"Uh huh. And what are you offering?" Rick asked.

"Well since this is an unproven movie, we're looking at $25,000 plus 5% if it hits 1 million dollars," Goomba said.

Rick looked over at me and crinkled his mouth and squeezed his eyes. I could tell that he didn't like that whatsoever.

"This is a proven book series with a serious following both on social media as well. You're going to have to do better than that," Rick said.

"I'd strongly reconsider if I were you," Goomba said.

"You want the exclusive international rights and all media. You own all rights in print, online, series and distribution. Plus, if you ever market something like escape rooms based on the books or what have you. Graham, let's go," Rick said.

"Wait a second. Alright, what if we made it $75,000?" Dexter asked.

Rick thought it over for a few minutes and then looked at me and shook his head.

"Gentlemen, I've done this for a living for thirty years. I'm pretty well known on the East Coast. Please give us a call if you're interested in seriously sitting down," Rick said as he stood up and motioned for us to get up, which we did.

"Gentlemen, we're here already. There's no reason to be like this. I'm sure we can come to some kind of agreement here," Goomba said. He punched the intercom for his assistant. "Ashley, would you please bring in a bottle of Blue and 5 glasses with ice please," he said as he sat back down.

Johnny Blue. Expensive. Not too expensive for him I'm sure, but I could see where this is going. Truth be told, without Rick I would have sold at 75.

"Here you go," Ashley said.

"Thank you dear. See yourself out please and hold my calls," Goomba said.

He poured us each about two shots worth in each glass and handed them to us.

"Cheers lady and gents," Goomba said.

Hannah put down her glass on the table. Rick took a sip. I downed my glass and motioned for more.

"A whiskey man eh?" Dexter asked.

"You could say that," I said.

"Alright, let's start this entire thing over. My name is Goomba, this is my associate Dexter. What is it that you are looking for exactly?" Goomba asked.

"For starters we want a commitment to the series," Rick stated.

"The best we can do is two. If the first one flops, then we'll have the ending wrapped up in the second," Dexter said.

"We want the right to add to the series and the right to revise," Rick said.

They looked at each other.

"What else?" Goomba asked as he poured me another glass, this time filling it up three quarters of the way.

"We want to retain the rights to this series," Rick said.

Again, they looked at each other. I had no idea what they were going to say, but I feel like they were letting

Rick just spew out demands and would address them later.

"Anything else?" Dexter asked.

"He's written four of them so far and is currently writing the fifth," Rick said.

"We know. Kid, to be honest with you, I'm a fan of your work. It's hard to see something new at my stage of the game, I've seen it all, but I like your style. Also, you and your friends are funny as hell. I've never really come across a funny thriller before," Goomba said.

"That's the thing we wanted to talk to you about," Dexter said.

"Yeah, what is that?" I asked.

"The ending. You need an ending to wrap this up," Dexter said.

"Also, we're going to want exclusive rights to distribute in all forms. We can make you an Executive Producer and give you script visibility if you're interested. That part is non-negotiable," Goomba said. "Also, we want the rights to all future works if we want them. We want the first right of refusal. Again, non-negotiable," Goomba said.

Rick looked at me and nodded.

"We want to make sure that the story stays true to its original nature. We don't want you going an opposite direction if you don't like how it came out. We all know what happened to Game of Thrones," Rick said.

"Hey, we had nothing to do with that," Dexter said.

"Understood," Rick said.

"Hey guys, what's your sales and marketing plan. I want to make sure you're going to treat my story with honor and not just buy it and shelve it forever. This is my legacy here. This is how people will remember me," I said as I took a big gulp of the Johnny.

Rick raised his eyebrows at me and smiled. I was starting to get a little bit of liquid confidence.

"I'm glad you asked. Now, we don't have anything formal yet, I hope you know that, but I can go over some basic stuff with you," Dexter said as he looked over to Goomba.

Goomba then spent the next 20 minutes refilling my glass and explaining their pitch. How they were going to market this as the greatest secret ever hidden from humanity. He told us about some outside of the box thinking that they had for this. I could tell that they legitimately prepared for this. I went to ask for another refill, but Hannah gave me evil eyes, so I finished my drink and put the cup down.

"Do you mind if I smoke in here?" I asked.

"Go right ahead, but please by the window. Ashley, please bring in an ashtray," Goomba said into his intercom.

Ashley came back in with an ashtray and handed it to me. I pulled out a cigarette and lit it up by the window. The first drag was so good. Nothing is better than a cigarette after a few drinks.

"Also, we want revision rights," Rick said.

They stopped and looked at each other, then back at Rick.

"This is going a bit far, don't you think?" Dexter asked.

"Gentlemen I just want to interject, I've got something to say," I said.

"Go on Graham," Goomba said.

"You're familiar with Blur Slanders correct?" I asked.

They nodded. "He's a loonbag," Dexter said.

"Maybe he is, it's possible. Here's the thing though. He talks about how the conservatives are being censored and that religion is dying in America. The Pledge of Allegiance is gone, and where it's not you can no longer say one nation under God, things of that nature," I said.

"Where are you going with this?" Dexter asked.

"Thanks for asking," I started as I took another large drag. I was definitely feeling the buzz with this cigarette,

Micah T. Dank

"The thing is, this is a rather mainstream view by conservatives. My politics aside, this is what they believe.
That they are being censored, that they are being muted,
removed from social media. The right clings to their
Religion and the left doesn't. Is that a fair assumption?" I
asked.

Goomba looked at me and took a cigar out of his
pocket and lit it up. "Interesting," he said.

"For years there has been a struggle between whether
religion is real. Whether it's good, or whether it's a lie
we've been fed. The left and the right fight over it all the
time. My books show a consistent flow of the last six
thousand years that religion is nothing more than star
worship. I believe if you make a movie series out of my
books, it can get to middle America and at the least start
questioning the things they believe in blindly. I know
Hollywood isn't conservative at all, that's never been a
big secret, but what if we put these out as a way to
logically show that Religion isn't real. I know people on
the coasts would love it, maybe not middle America, but
who knows. There's a reason why no Atheists books
become movies, yet at the same time you have religious
movies all the time. If you've read my stories, you must
know how much nonsense religion is, and I have the
logic behind it," I said as I started breathing a little
heavier. I need to not drink so fast.

The two men looked at each other and started whispering to one another.

Just then my phone rang. I should have left it on silent. I answered the call from a number I didn't recognize. After a short conversation I looked up.

"Can you summarize what you just said to me again," I asked.

"Sure, no problem," the voice on the other line began, "We loved your book series. I'm Mike from AquaStream videos and we want to make a short series out of your books. We'll offer you $250,000 up front for the rights. We can talk about it more if you're interested. I'll email you our information and set up a meeting," he said.

"Thank you. I will talk to you soon. Look forward to that email," I said and hung up the phone.

"Do you mind giving us the room for a few minutes," Goomba said.

"Not at all," Rick said as he stood up and buttoned his suit. We walked outside and I started pacing.

"Did they ask you to leave?" Ashley asked.

"No, they just needed the room for a few minutes," I said.

"That's a good sign. Usually they just kick people out," Ashley said as she smiled to me.

After a few minutes, Dexter came back outside.

"Goomba wants to talk, but only to Graham," Dexter said.

"That's ridiculous, come on guys let's . . ." Rick said as I cut him off.

"It's OK, I got this," I said.

I walked back in with Dexter and sat down at the table. I motioned for him to give me another taste of the whiskey, which he did.

"Your pitch was pretty great, you should be proud of yourself kid. For too many years religion has had secular people's number and nothing gets better. After reading your books, I've come to the conclusion that we need to move past religion in order to evolve more. That being said here's what we're going to do. I'll give you 7% for anything over 1 million dollars and 5 percent for anything over 10. I'll also give you half a million, but that includes the rights to all your books. Depending on how this movie does, we'll revisit future. But this offer is only valid right now. Once you walk out the door, it's gone," Goomba said.

I looked at him. That was a ton of money, but giving them exclusive rights to all my material. Ah screw it, I was in a giddy mood.

"Deal," I said as I shook his hand and Dexter's hand.

"Excellent. You can take the rest of the bottle home with you. I hope you're not driving," Goomba asked.

"No, believe it or not I feel great," I said.

"That's good to hear. You'll receive some paperwork in the mail shortly," Dexter said as he shook my hand again.

"One more thing Graham. Do you have a title for the movie?" Goomba asked.

"Inside the Rabbit Hole," I said.

"Right but the subtitle," he asked.

"Beneath the Veil," I said.

"Excellent," Goomba said.

I went outside and smiled at Hannah and Rick. It wasn't until we got in the car that I told them I closed a million-dollar picture. Hannah screamed and Rick patted me on the back.

"Glad I could help," Rick said.

Just as we were about to pull away and go celebrate some, I got a call from Rosette. I let it go to voicemail. She called Hannah. Hannah picked up.

"What's up girl, you'll never guess what just happened," she said to the phone.

"Let me talk to Graham please girl, love you," Rosette said.

Hannah handed me the phone.

"Graham, I don't know how to break this to you so I'm just going to say it, but your mother passed away a few minutes ago," she said.

I dropped the phone on the floor. Then I blacked out.

Life contains but two tragedies. One is not to get your heart's desire; the other is to get it—Socrates

Chapter Four

We landed at Logan after taking the Red Eye back. Speaking of red eye, my eyes were bloodshot from crying the entire time on the flight. I basically curled up into a ball and had Hannah rubbing my head the entire time. I knew this was coming. My mother never really took care of herself. She drank more than I ever could and did it much longer, it's a miracle she lasted as long as she did. We got out with a surprise though. Everyone was there to meet us in that Scooby Doo van that we still had. I learned that Jean just bought it outright in the event something ever came up and we all needed to go somewhere.

"How you doing, Newson?" Rosette asked as she gave me a big hug.

"I've definitely had better days," I said.

"How you holding up, brother?" Jackson asked.

"It's been rough. But am I glad to see all of you," I said.

Lastly Jean and Larisa came up to me and didn't say a word. They just gave me a big hug. This one hit me especially hard for some reason. I just sat there, arms down while they wrapped around me.

"Come on, let's get you home and dressed for the funeral. Jean took care of all the arrangements," Rosette said.

I turned to Jean. He nodded.

"Je suis tres desole mon ami. I paid for everything already. All you have to do is go home and put on a suit and we'll go," he said.

"My mother wanted to be buried, not cremated," I replied.

"I know. I remember hearing her talk about it. I got a plot at Blue Hill for her," he said and smiled.

Blue Hill Cemetery was in Braintree, one town over on the T train. But we would probably take the giant shagwagon that we now own apparently.

Most of the day was a blur to me. We got home, I microdosed, and took a 45-minute hot shower. I'm not one to take a while doing trivial things, but I really needed this one. When I got out, Hannah had laid out all the clothes for me. I put on my black suit. It still fits. That's a good thing. We then made our way to the funeral home.

Walking into a funeral home for a viewing of your mother is not something I recommend. The second I saw her, I just lost it. It wasn't so much that she was gone, or pale, or cold, it was how peaceful and happy she looked. That lady had demons in her life that she was fighting, and it didn't matter how hard it was for her, she always made sure I had what I needed, and encouraged me in everything I did. Leaving med school was a hard pill for her to swallow, but she saw how happy I was and how I was able to support myself doing what I love, and I think in the end she came around. I had lost my dad almost fifteen years prior, and I don't really remember much of it. This time it was much different. I looked at my mother and the rosary beads that were wrapped around her hand, and I just shook my head and turned to my friends, not really sure what to say.

"Did you guys know that in the year 100 AD, the Old Testament's canon was not complete officially. Much like the Catholic council that put together the books of the New Testament, the Old Testament needed the same treatment. There was a council in Jamnia, where the wise men met. The only problem was there was a Gospel written 30 years prior called Mark. Canonizing the Jewish Bible, this is literally where Judaism and Christianity split. There were open discussions about whether or not to include Jesus in the Old Testament, but after a long deliberation they decided against it. It was very close to having the Old and New Testament, one long testament. Just think what would have happened if the savior predicted in the Book of Micah, was included in the Old Testament as well. There wouldn't be such division in people," I said as I turned back and fidgeted with her Rosary. I started to feel my blood boil.

"She came from a different time period, Graham. This isn't how she was raised," Hannah said.

"It's how I was raised, and we were able to figure all this out," I snapped back.

"Well maybe times are a changing now, but she was a devotee, so try not to take it personally," Jackson said.

I turned and nodded to him. He was right of course. I was taking my anger out on them for losing her. Everyone was well aware of this, which is why they were giving me such leeway with my actions.

"Excuse me sir, which one of you is Graham Newsdon?" The owner asked.

"That's me," I said as I stood up and wiped the tears away from my face.

"There are some reporters outside that would like to speak with you," he said.

"What now?" I replied.

"Should I make them go away?" the man asked.

"No, it's fine. Jackson, Jean, come with me," I said as I turned to go to the door.

I opened the door outside where it was California like sunny. I squinted as I turned to focus on the reporters. I heard a bunch of cameras clicking and they all started speaking at once. What was going on.

"One at a time. What is this?" I asked.

"Graham, just taking a picture for the local news. I'm sorry to bother you," the man said.

I finally was able to focus and saw that it was Peter from the Zip Code Bandits. They must be doing a local story about death in the town.

"Excuse me Graham, hi, this is Tom from TMZ," the man said.

"Did you just say TMZ?" I asked bewildered. What the hell were they doing here?

"I'm sorry for your loss Graham. I just wanted to know, do you have a comment on the Westboro Baptist Church's claim?" Tom asked.

"What claim?" I turned to him.

Tom frowned, I don't think he expected I had no clue what he was talking about.

"Westboro Baptist Church claims that because you included them in your books, that your mother's death was retribution from God," Tom said.

"They said what?!" I screeched.

"Do you have a comment?" Tom asked. "Incidentally, they are planning on protesting your mother's funeral at the Cemetery," he finished.

I couldn't believe what I was hearing. I opened my mouth to reply, and Jean spoke before I could.

"No comment. Come on Graham, let's go back inside," Jean said as we turned around to go in.

"Can I just get a comment for the record?" Tom asked as he tried to walk inside. Jackson took a step to the left and blocked him. Looking at the size of Jackson, Tom decided it's better off not to be shredded into strands of string cheese.

We went back inside and caught up with the girls. I explained to them everything that happened. Hannah just walked up to me and gave me a hug.

"Come on sweetie, let's get out of here. We can beat them to the cemetery," she said. I nodded.

We walked out the back of the funeral parlor because the reporter was still in the front and loaded into the van. Jean started driving over to the Cemetery. I pulled out a cigarette from my pocket and lit it up, rolled down the window.

"Ay, tu ne peut pas fumer ici!" Jean screeched.

"Did a French guy just tell me I can't smoke in his creepy van?" I asked.

Everyone laughed. If there's one piece of advice I can give to the world, it's never lose your sense of humor.

"You won't be laughing when my special toy comes in," Jean said.

We all looked at him.

"You're what now?" I asked.

"I bought something really cool, it hasn't shipped from New York yet, but it's very expensive and I intend on using it while we're all out on my boat," he said.

"Is it a parasailing thingy?" Rosette asked.

"Not quite, but you're close," he said as he winked at her.

We got to the cemetery and sat in the van and talked until the funeral people arrived. I got caught up on how everybody was doing, what we missed while we were on our honeymoon. I also told them about the pitch from Venus Lair Studios and what they wanted to do with my book series.

"You do know that if you turn these into movies, what privacy you thought you had, what you just experienced back there, that's just the beginning," Rosette said.

"People have been put to death for way less than the kind of things we've learned, experienced. This is a real chance to get true history out into the open. I'm willing to sacrifice that," I said.

"What about your wife though? It's not just you anymore," Jackson asked.

"I'll support him in whatever he does," Hannah said.

"Well I guess that's settled then," Jackson said.

"There's one more thing though," I said.

"What is it?" Jean asked.

"Remember in my second book when I bugged out and went to the bar and ran into the Westboro Baptist Church?" I asked.

"Yeah," Rosette said.

"I emailed the studio and asked if they would let me play the bartender when they got up to that in the movies," I laughed.

"That's pretty ironic considering what we just heard," Rosette laughed.

"I know it sounds stupid, but I used to act in high school. I want my freakin SAG card," I said and laughed.

We all laughed for a few minutes until we saw a ton of cars pull up. Black Lincolns. I was wondering if that was the funeral procession, but then one by one these assholes got out of the cars with their picket signs and started forming a barrier along the outside. They weren't allowed in and they knew it, but they could sure make this impossible for us to have this in peace.

"Remember Jackson, most of them are lawyers. That's how they fund these trips. They entice, someone hits them, they get sued, they get paid, they have funding again. Do not, under any circumstance hit them," I said.

"What about lighting them on fire?" Jackson asked.

I laughed.

We talked for another 45 minutes until finally the procession arrived.

We got out of the Van and made our way to the plot that Jean had bought. It was against the wall. My mother would have loved the peace and quiet, and most importantly, being away from other people. I smiled. It's great to have friends like this. The only problem was that the protesters were on the other side of the wall. I looked over the ledge and saw them all starting to curse at me. I also saw Tom, from TMZ, taking pictures of them. I pulled my phone out and called the police. Within 15 minutes they were down. They couldn't make them go away, but they were able to push them a little further back. Finally, the priest arrived.

It was a lovely service, despite the nonsense going on outside the walls. We all spoke, it was nice to hear my friends recall moments that my mother touched their hearts. Finally. it was time to lower her down. This brought me back to when I was watching James being lowered in the ground. I was the last one left of my family, and this thought hit me hard. I was going to have a drink when I got back home. After she was lowered in the ground, the Priest handed me the shovel, and I put the first patch of dirt into the ground. I handed the shovel off to Jackson and grabbed Jean's keys and walked back to the car. I was done.

While God waits for his temple to be built of love,
Men bring stones—Rabindranath Tagore

Chapter Five

We got to our house and I poured myself a gin and tonic. Jean had left a bottle of gin last time he came over with Larisa. This was the elephant in the room, but nobody was going to say anything to me today after what I had just been through. Everyone joined in actually. We sat there and cheersed to my mom and we sipped our drinks. We left the TV on. Blur was on. He was talking about how the US Military wants to put brain chips in people that converts their electric pulses and thoughts to binary code. I turned the TV off. Little did I know we were going to need to understand binary code shortly.

I walked into my room and sat down on my bed and had my glass of gin with a splash of tonic. Rosette followed in after me.

"You're familiar with Erik Erikson's levels, right?" she asked.

"I am," I said.

"Industry vs. Inferiority. You lost your father during that time frame which really matured you. You started burying yourself in school and learning because it grounded you. You wanted to master everything, you worked so hard while your mom stayed home and drank herself. It's known that people who were victims of abuse when they were younger tend to abuse when they're older. When you discovered it at 14, you felt like it brought you closer to your mother. Though you hated it. The way you've described how you feel when you drink worries me," she said.

"Don't psychoanalyze me right now Rose. Now's not the time," I said.

"Fine, but when you're done with all of this, I want to give you the Minnesota Personality Test," she said.

"For what?" I asked.

"I'll tell you after I give it to you. Just tell me that you'll take it," she said.

"That's fine," I said.

"Also, I want you to stop microdosing. That's not a long-term solution. At least try TMS," she said.

"Tanscranial Magnetic Stimulation?" I asked.

She nodded.

"I'll consider it," I said as I took another giant sip of my drink and shuttered. This juice is making my nipples hard.

"Maybe when your movies come out, you can run for office one day," she said and laughed.

"Do you realize what my Overton window would look like?" I said and laughed.

"Come back out with us, we need you here with us, not buried away in your room," she said.

"Alright, just give me a second," I said.

She left and I went to my dresser and opened the top drawer. There was a framed picture of my family together. I must have been six. I have very vague memories of this day, but it's basically the only good picture I've ever had in my entire life with my complete family. I put it away and walked back into the living room, not expecting to run into the problem at hand.

I grabbed Larisa's computer that I was using to write my books. As my books were quite the controversy, I had been using her locked down computer to make sure that nobody could access my writings. I went to open my latest book I was writing, and a message came up saying that it was locked. Suddenly the screen went down and came back up with a chilling message:

If you want access to this and it not to be spread all over the dark web, please pay 1,000,000 in Bitcoin.

"Larisa!!!" I screamed.

"What?" she said.

"Come here," I said.

"Oh God Graham, what did you do? Did you open an email recently on this computer?" she asked.

"I did, it said, "Venus Lair Studios Contract" and I opened it. So?" I asked.

"It wasn't from them. You have to check where it came from. This is Ransomware," she said.

"I don't understand," I replied.

"Hold on a second," she began as she nervously started typing on her computer at lightning speed, "I've seen this one before," she said.

"Seen what?" I asked.

"A few years back there was a wave of these types of things that ran through the NSA in Maryland. Something called EternalBlue. These hackers had frozen thousands of computers and messed up a ton of services. Many surgeries had to be postponed. They asked for money. It basically exploited a vulnerability in the Microsoft SMB protocol. The NSA knew about it, but kept their mouth shut. Microsoft said it was fixed, but not everybody downloaded and installed the fixes. Then something called WannaCry came out that infected the NHS. Fuck, I thought I had a VPN or a proxy in place. I can't remember, I put it in so long ago. I know I had 'Hide-MyAss' at one point," she said.

"Hide your what?" Rosette asked.

"It's a popular proxy. It might have been a VPN though. Someone must have broken the encryption. Fuck, I knew I should have kept up with this," she said.

"What does this mean then?" I asked.

"It means that if you want access to these files, we're going to have to pay the ransom," she said.

"There has to be another way!" I yelled.

"Unfortunately, from where I'm sitting there's not. Wait, hold on a sec," she said as she stared at her computer. I came around and looked at the computer as well. The mouse was moving on its own. Someone was in her computer as we spoke. I watched them open a brand new Word Doc file. Chillingly, they started typing on the blank page.

Do I have your attention now, Graham Newsdon?

I sat there frozen for a second. By instinct, Larisa grabbed a piece of tape from the desk behind her from the scotch tape roll and put it over her camera on her computer, then took a black marker and blacked out over the camera. She then hooked her computer to the new 75-inch flat screen TV that Hannah and I were gifted for our wedding. Within seconds, the screen was flooded with this document.

Verily I say to thee, that blacking out the camera is the least of your worries dear.

What do you want? Larisa typed back.

You think that the computer is the only thing that was hacked? Please. I can see all of you through your TV right now. I'm in your dishwasher, your Alexa,

your security system, your nest thermostat, hell, I can even hack your pink rabbit Larisa.

"What the hell is the pink rabbit?" I asked.

Then without missing a beat this person wrote back.

Her vibrator.

"You can hack a vibrator?" Jean asked bewildered. I think he was just as confused by that as the fact that she even owned one. What was lost on him was the fact that we didn't have to type to him in order for him to hear us. He was in our house.

Hello Larisa, tell me dear, is Professor MacDonald still teaching at MIT?

"No he's not," she replied.

That's such a shame. Anyways I see you all here now, which is a good thing. I wanted to tell you Graham how much I admire you and your work. You've come such a long way. All your hard work has finally paid off and you're going to be known all over the world. Is that what you really want?

"Few seek wisdom for *its* own sake; Most desire it only as a solution to the discomforts of life. While wisdom certainly releases a man from bondage to trivial annoyances, it also bestows upon him a larger responsibility than he ever knew. That's Manly P. Hall. I'll do what I have to do to reach as many people as I can. I don't care what happens to me or my life at this point," I replied.

I admire your honesty. A bit foolish, but truly you are pure. Anyway, let's get right to it. I'm actually not your enemy. Quite the opposite actually. With everything going on in your life, the only way to make a proper entrance is by making a splash. I think that I have, and that I have all your attention now.

"What is it that you want? Whoever you are," I asked.

Who I am is not important, who we are is. You can call us 'the ones who keep the balance.' When something is at a 5, to counter it should be a -5. Zero is perfect harmony. We strive to keep things at Zero. But lately, there has been a serious disadvantage to us. There are many who are out to steal as much of the resources that they can in this world. There are billionaires who are having 5-6 heart replacement surgeries, while stymieing research for stem cell research into growing new hearts. Which brings me to my next point actually. I know you have been made aware of the library of Alexandria having been moved. Well, we had the initial location to it, there is wisdom and information in there from civilizations that aren't even a thought in today's world. The world is not ready for that yet, yet someone found our

location and killed everyone protecting it. We need your help locating it again and giving us the coordinates so we can protect it.

I sat there and thought up a reply, opened my mouth but no words came out. Why did this have to fall on me. Was he right about me being foolish? I wouldn't be as anonymous as I sort of am now to be able to do this much longer. Maybe that's what he meant. "What's in this for us?" I asked.

You get first crack at the information in there. Whatever you find, you can include in your next book. Unfortunately, when they moved the Library against our wishes, they destroyed the catalogue of all writings that we had, so nobody is quite sure exactly what's there. It needs to be done up again. Like I said, it's yours for the picking. Also, the people we are dealing with are very unrefined. They don't speak in the Bible in the same sense that you're used to. They speak in the texts that were left out of the Bible. You will have to acclimate yourself to that knowledge quickly if you are to be of use to us.

"How will I know where to begin?" I asked.

The only thing we were able to ascertain from these people was the following code. 24610010. They said it is 'buried and will serve you well'. I have unlocked your files on your computer, but I am

staying logged into your computer so we can still communicate. I wish you luck.

Just like that he stopped typing and we were left to our own thoughts. I stood up and went into the bedroom.

"Where are you going?" Hannah asked.

"I just needed to grab this," I said as I flashed a book.

"What is that?" Jackson asked.

"It's a book I've been meaning to start but need to now. It's the Complete Apocrypha," I said.

"Well, what are we supposed to do?" Rosette asked.

"Figure out the riddle," I said as I sat down and began to read.

I would not read that long as we soon would be able to figure out what it is. Truth is, I didn't need to have that kind of knowledge as someone incredibly versed in it would come to our aid. I just didn't realize how balls deep into the rabbit hole we were going to go this time.

To learn who rules over you, simply find out who you are not allowed to criticize—Voltaire

If anyone can show me, and prove to me, that I am wrong in thought or deed, I will gladly change. I seek the truth, which never yet hurt anybody. It is only persistence in self-delusion and ignorance which does harm—Marcus Aurelius

Chapter Six

"Well, that entire ordeal was exciting," Hannah said.

"Easy, he might still be listening. Are you still there?" I asked.

We got no answer after about a 5-minute wait. It didn't seem like he was interested in listening to our day-to-day. He was just going to be there to check in on us once in a while. We were going to have to get used to that.

"Alright guys, so what's that code again?" Jackson asked.

"24610010," Rosette replied.

"Thank you, sweetheart," Larisa said. Rosette giggled.

"What is it with you two flirting all the time?" I asked. Jean's eyes got wide.

"I'm not sure. Rosette seems like she'd be a good time," Larisa said and winked at her. Rosette blushed and giggled again.

"Can I give you the Kinsey Scale?" Rosette asked Larisa.

"Only if I can give it to you when we're done," Larisa said and smiled at Rosette.

"Alright enough you two. Any ideas on the code?" I asked.

"Let me look into it, hold on," Larisa said as she started typing away at her newly released computer. She had full access once again.

"It says online that it's a Ferrari part," Larisa said.

"That's clearly not it," I replied.

"Any suggestions?" Larisa turned and asked me.

"What if the 10010 is binary for something?" Jackson asked.

"10010 is 18 in binary code," Larisa replied.

"18 again? Like that other code that I broke," Rosette said in a proud moment.

"That can't be it. Can we separate the numbers individually?" I asked.

"2 4 6 1 0 0 1 0," Larisa typed on the screen. She then got up and switched the connection to the tv and put it on the big screen.

"I'm at a loss for this," I said.

"This was one of the trickier ones we've come across. We were all stumped. I stepped outside to have a cigarette. I don't like smoking in my own house. Go figure. Rosette followed me outside.

"Hi pup," she said.

"Hey kitten," I replied.

"Listen, I'm sorry I came at you the way I did the day of your mom's thing. Truth is, I'm just really worried about you. If you ever need to talk, I'll be here to talk.

"Thanks sweets. Means a lot. And yes, I will take your test when this is all done," I said.

I walked back into the house after my cigarette and met everyone. Hannah had run to the bathroom as she had gotten sick, and we could all hear her throwing up in there.

"What did that girl eat or drink?" Jackson asked.

"No clue, but hopefully she feels better," I said.

She came out of the bathroom holding her stomach. She went into the kitchen and grabbed some Pepto from the fridge and chugged it down. She turned to me and smiled as she walked back down to us and sat down on the couch.

"Sorry about that," she said.

"No worries lovebug," I said.

"Guys, the code," Larisa said.

"What if it's a coordinate on the map. Or a star. We know this is always about astronomy and astrology, right?" Rosette asked.

Larisa searched the web for it, there was nothing.

"Ok so it's not that. What if it's backmasked?" I asked.

"What's that?" Hannah asked, still feeling a little queasy.

"Backwards. Like the musicians that put messages in their songs when you play them in reverse, maybe this is in reverse too," I said.

"What would make you think of that?" Jackson asked.

"Because we're running out of ideas," I said.

"There is nothing with 01001642," Larisa said.

"Come on guys, we're better than this," Jean finally chimed in.

I grabbed the laptop from Larisa and punched in the binary code again. For some reason I was stuck on that possibly being it. Then something came up that gave me an idea. 10010 was a zip code for Chelsea in Manhattan.

"We've been to Manhattan a few times already. Maybe the secret is there," I said.

"Well what about 246?" Jackson asked.

"Maybe it's an address," I said.

"Well what about a block and cross strcct. Need those to find anything in the concrete jungle," Jackson said.

Then an idea hit me.

"What if 246 is the address. What if it's 24th and 6th? I asked. "Larisa, pull up what's at that location," I said.

Larisa started typing away at her computer as we watched her screen. All of a sudden, we froze when we found out what was at the corner of 24th and 6th. It's the New York FreeMasons lodge chapter.

"You've got to be kidding me," Jackson said.

"Good job Newsdon," Rosette said.

"What was the other part of it?" I asked.

"Something about buried and served us well," Hannah said.

"Well what the actual hell guys. Are we supposed to dig up underneath the Masonic lodge for a clue? We'll never get in there," Rosette said.

"Chill. Look, maybe it's cryptic for something else. Could the serve me well and buried mean something is buried in a server in there?" I asked.

Everybody stopped and looked at me at once like I was the one that put these clues forward.

"I'm trying to pull up the blueprints of this place and videos et cetera, et cetera, et cetera. Nothing is coming up. This place is locked down. If there is a server in there, I don't know where it is, or what's protecting it," Larisa said.

We gave Larisa a half an hour to get this figured out, but she had no luck. I had an idea, but I didn't want to use it yet. To be honest, I might get screamed at if I tried to use it.

"I got a list of emails for the Lodge. I was able to get in their emails and check for any suspicious activity. We're going to need to physically go there and go ghost the server in order to find out what's buried in there," Larisa said.

We gave her another hour to go through people's emails until she finally found something.

"Here's something. There's an email that went out from a man named Jim about a 3rd degree initiate saying that he's expecting a call for . . ." Larisa stopped reading and started giggling.

"A call for what?" I asked.

"It's his initiation party, and he wants two furries to come with alcohol," she said as she broke out into a fit of laughter.

"Qu-est que c'est un furry?" Jean asked.

We all stopped and looked at him and all started laughing.

"You know those people who dress up like sexualized animals. Remember when NP was talking to us about the sexualization of animals a lifetime ago? Remember Bunny and Kitty?" Rosette asked him, wiping tears away from her eyes.

"Quoi?!" he asked bewildered.

"This is our in guys, I'm going to give him a call about this right now," Larisa said as she took her cell phone and punched in his phone number.

"So Jackson, what exactly are you working on these days?" I asked.

"I've been writing a paper on bio-centrism," he replied.

"What exactly is that?" Hannah asked.

"It's basically a principle that says that consciousness is fundamental, and that what we perceive as matter is only there because consciousness is there to experience it," he said.

We stared at him. He was always working on some crazy theory to teach the brilliant young minds of the future.

"I'm going to look into it, sounds interesting," I said.

"Really?!" he asked bewildered.

"Yeah," I said.

"There's so much I can talk to you about the Lanza model," He began before I cut him off.

"Another time, not now Jax," I said.

"Fair enough," he said.

"Hey guys, so here's the deal. I spoke to Jim. The guy's name is Andrew, and he's being initiated in 2 days. He's going to tell the security that we're coming. I told him we're 'T Dog Entertainment' and we will take care of everything. By the way, this is going to be one kink-fest," she said.

"Why T Dog Entertainment?" I asked.

"I dunno. Furries, this came to mind. I have to go and get a few costumes for us in Weymouth and pick up this old ice cream cart they're selling in Hull. I'll be back in a little. Jean, the keys please," Larisa said.

Jean tossed the keys across the room. Larisa did a little spin and caught the keys, then curtsied and blew a kiss at Rosette. Once again, Rosette giggled.

"Why an ice cream cart?" I asked.

"They probably have a metal detector and a full body scan. I need to get some of my devices in there, which reminds me I need to get some black balloons also," Larisa said.

I wasn't quite sure what devices she meant or why we needed it, but I nudged her off. We sat there and talked for a little while, and I turned on the TV, Blur was on again. This time he was talking about the Black Knight Satellite that's in our orbit. I turned the TV off. I don't know why I do this to myself anymore.

Larisa came back a few hours later with everything in the van. She brought the costumes in. She brought three, one for her, one for me and one for Jackson, in case we needed any muscle in there. We all tried them on and modeled them for the rest. Everybody was in hysterics by the time we took the costumes off.

"What if they try to do anything sexual with you?" Jean asked worried.

"I can handle myself sweetie," Larisa said. "However, there is one thing that's bothering me. We don't know where the server room is. There's not going to be a lot of time for us to be able to get this done, and I can't for the life of me locate it. Graham, that thing you didn't want to do, we're going to need you to do it."

"This could backfire tremendously," I said.

"I don't care, we need this. So please make the call," Larisa said.

I turned away from them and dialed a phone number into my phone. It rang 3 times, and then finally someone picked up the line.

"Hello?" the voice said.

"Hi Josh, long time," I began to my old Washington, DC Mason friend.

The one who follows the crowd will usually go no further than the crowd. The one who walks alone is likely to find himself in places no one has ever been before
—Albert Einstein

Chapter Seven

"Been a long time, Graham. How's everything," he said. I could tell he was busy and wouldn't have a long time to talk.

"Nothing much, just about to throw a party in the City," I said.

"Oh yeah? And where exactly will that be?" he asked.

"24th and 6th in Chelsea. You know it?" I asked.

The line went silent for a moment.

"Graham, what the hell have you gotten yourself into this time?" he asked.

"I'm sorry Josh. I really wish there was another way, but we desperately need your help," I said.

"What do you need from me? Why is it that every time we talk, I could end up losing my position?" he asked.

"I'm sorry Josh. I wish there was another way," I said.

"What do you need? And what exactly are you doing at the Masons hall?" he asked.

"I told you, we're throwing a party for a new 3rd degree," I said.

"Uh huh and tell me Graham, the second you step into there and they see who you are, how exactly are you going to make it out of there?" he asked.

"I'll be in a Pikachu suit, so that won't be a problem," I said fighting back the urge to laugh.

The line went silent again.

"Graham, I have no idea what you're doing, but I can't be a part of this. I told you a while back I couldn't. The fact that you mentioned me in your book series got me in a ton of hot water with the Lodge in D.C. What exactly is it that you need from me?" he asked.

I figured I shouldn't beat around the bush anymore, that I had to tell him what was going down.

"There is a secret code buried within their server," I said.

"Oh really, and you expect to just go into the server room and rip it off. You're not going to get into it. First of all, it's locked up and protected by a Faraday cage," Josh said.

I paused for a minute.

"Jax, what's a Faraday cage?" I asked.

"It keeps electric impulses from reaching what's in there. It diffuses the electricity around the entire cage so that what's inside is protected. Ever seen a man in a cage and a bolt of lightning hits it and he's fine. That's what he's in. Why do you ask?" Jackson asked.

I turned back to the phone. "Look Josh, we don't have a lot of time," I said.

"I'm sorry Graham but, like I said, I can't have any part of this," he said.

"Josh, the Library of Alexandria exists. It was moved," I said, dropping the hammer.

The line was silent for a minute.

"I'm going to call you back in a minute from my burner phone," Josh said and he hung up.

I waited for Josh to call back and turned to Jackson. "Jax, you're going to have to help us figure out how to get into that Faraday cage. We need to ghost the server, and we're not going to have a lot of time to do it."

"Working up some ideas boss," Jackson said.

Finally, after 2 long minutes my phone rang.

"Did you say that the Library of Alexandria is still around?" Josh asked. I could hear his eyes get wide from the other end of the line.

"Yes," I said.

"How do you know for sure?" he asked.

"I was told by an entity," I said.

"An entity? Like what kind of entity?" he asked.

I pressed the urge to tell him it's an out of world entity, but instead I said "They call themselves those who keep the balance. Do you believe me or not?" I asked.

"Did you say those that keep the balance?" He froze. I could tell that struck a chord with him. "It's not a matter of believing you or not. I know you've been into some deep stuff before. But why would the Library have been hidden all these years?" he asked.

"I was told it was because the information in it would evolve us as a planetary race ten times more than where we are at right now. It would once and for all destroy religion and possibly connect us with the gods," I said.

I could hear he was starting to breathe more heavily on the other line. The allure of being part of this was starting to be too much for Josh to control.

"I could lose everything I've built for myself for helping you. What exactly do you need from me?" he asked.

"I need to know where the server room to the Masons Lodge on 24th and 6th is," I said.

Josh was silent for about 30 seconds. Finally he said, "I have to go," and hung up the phone.

"Well baby, did he tell you?" Hannah asked.

"Not exactly. We don't exactly have enough time to figure out where it is before . . ." I paused as I got a text message.

I opened the text message and saw that it was from an anonymous website that you couldn't trace.

Back elevator, 9th floor.

"Well?" Rosette asked.

"We're going to the city again," I said as everyone started packing up their stuff. Jean made reservations at the Holiday Inn on 24th. We were going to have to set up shop. Larisa was still in the back room filling up balloons and unpacking the boxes of liquor that she bought for the ice cream cart. Little did we know the depravity we would see once we were inside the lodge. Also, the chain of events that I started with Josh would end up changing both our lives permanently.

Masonry, like all the religions, all the mysteries, hermeticism, and alchemy, conceals its secrets from all except the adepts and sages, or the elect, and uses false explanations and misinterpretations of its symbols to mislead those who deserve only to be mislead; to conceal the truth—Albert Pike

To come then at once to the point, Masonry is derived and is the remains of, the religion of the ancient Druids; who like the magi of Persia and the priests of Heliopolis in Egypt, were Priests of the Sun. They paid worship to this great luminary, as the cause visible agent of a great invisible first cause, whom they styled, time without limits—Thomas Paine

Chapter Eight

"I hate Manhattan traffic. I mean really, is there anything worse?" I asked.

"Boston traffic during the Marathon," Rosette replied.

"She's got a point, sweetie," Hannah said.

I looked over at Hannah. I just smiled. It was not that long ago that she was infected with a brain parasite that was literally keeping her alive. I was hoping there was no lasting or permanent damage done to her, but so far it doesn't seem to be that way. Many people live with Toxo for much of their lives without knowing any better. I was just hoping that we wouldn't go through that hell again.

"Turn left here," I said. We just passed Penn a few minutes ago. We turned down 24th.

Larisa turned left. "So what's the game plan guys? We have a few hours to kill before our big date. What's the deal?" she asked as she honked her horn and slammed on the brakes.

"Yup, New York City traffic. We're home," I joked. "Anyway, the plan is to check into the hotel and go over the plan," I said.

We had the back window open because Larisa bought a ton of dry ice to keep the liquor frozen cold and, as dry ice sublimates, it displaces the oxygen with carbon dioxide in the air. None of us wanted to pass out and crash over a bridge inception style.

We pulled into the parking garage under the hotel and went in. Jean took care of the reservations. He had it under his uncle's name, so we got the discount. He happened to be out of the City this week, so we were able to cash in on that. We brought the duffle bags upstairs as well as the rest of the balloons. We got situated in our giant suite and turned the TV on. Blur was on TV again, and I can't tell you what he was talking about this time because it could get me killed if I brought it up. Let's just say that the Royal family has some legal problems that are hidden from the world. I turned the TV off and poured myself a drink.

"Are you sure that's such a good idea babe?" Hannah looked at me.

"Baby, I need to loosen up for this. This is sick and twisted and I need to be cool as ice. I'm just having one, albeit a big one. Don't worry," I said.

"Fine Newsdon, now everyone put your earpieces on, we need to test them," Rosette said.

I took a sip of my drink and put the earpiece on and went into the bathroom.

"Testing, 1 2 3 4," I said.

"We hear you honey," Hannah said.

"Jax and Riss. You guys reading me?" I said.

"Roger that homeslice," Jackson said.

"I'm plugged in," Larisa said.

"OK good. Since the three of us are going in alone, the rest of you need to stay in the hotel and make sure that everything goes well," I said.

We went over the plan. The plan was to basically hop out of the van at the freight entrance of the building with the liquor and the balloons. The balloons Larisa told me would serve a double purpose. Some of them would have materials in them that we need for the extraction and to make sure everything goes smoothly. I had to ask what she had planned.

"Riss, what do you have in these balloons?" I asked.

"Well they're going to scan us up and down as well as the balloons. As soon as the balloons scan and come back that there's metal in them, I'm going to pop the front one and a pair of fuzzy handcuffs are going to fall down from them. They should let us go at that point. Now in the balloon to the back is a USB kill stick. It looks just like a flash drive, but what it does is when you plug it into a server or a computer, it builds up an electrical charge in it, then when it's full it discharges the electricity in a large burst back into the electric component in question. Completely fries the entire system," she said.

"Why do we want to fry the system?" I asked.

"Because I've been looking into what kind of setup they have there, and there's no way I can with the time we have NOT leave a fingerprint that something was done to it. I don't want it backtracked to us," she said.

"Oh, I said. Well, what's in the rest of the balloons?" I asked.

"That, oh just dumb stuff. Condoms, Finger traps, KY, that sort of stuff," she said.

"You planning on getting lucky tonight?" Jean asked with a tinge of jealousy.

"No, but I am hoping that if we get them drunk enough, they'll let me handcuff them to the chair and that should buy us enough time to get to the server room," Larisa said. "But thanks for worrying about me boo boo."

"Also, Graham, I found out something. Did you know the tin foil hat that makes the conspiracy theorists headgear, that comes directly from a Faraday cage?" Jackson said.

"That's interesting. I didn't know that," I said.

We sat around the room for another hour and a half, and then finally the sun started to go down. It was showtime. We put on our costumes and tested our earpieces one more time. Good as gold. We went into the elevator and took it to the basement where the cars were. We got in the van, Jean was driving. It was literally down the block from it, but truth be told, even for NYC, 3 furries pushing an ice cream cart full of liquor with kinky balloons might be too much for Chelsea. We said our goodbyes and jumped out of the van and pushed the service entry button. Nobody came after a minute. I slammed on it and slammed on the door. Finally, I heard steps coming our way and some mumbling. When the door opened, the doorman was not expecting what he saw and just burst out laughing.

"So you're here for Andrew, right?" he asked, still giggling.

We nodded our heads.

"What's a matter, don't you guys talk?" he asked confused.

We shook our head no.

"What's in the cart?" he asked.

I lifted it open and there was smoke from the dry ice.

"What the hell is that?" he asked as he started to radio for help.

With ninja reflexes, Jackson grabbed his head and put it in the cooler. The man struggled for a minute and then passed out from the carbon dioxide. Jackson then picked him up and brought him inside and put him on the floor with the radio on his chest. He took his glasses off his face and put them on a ledge that he couldn't see.

"What did you do that for?" I asked.

"Relax, he's not even going to remember what happened. Just that he got dizzy. After he finds his glasses, whenever that will be, he will just go back to work or bang out the rest of the night," Jackson said.

I shrugged my shoulders and we walked inside and got to the elevator. Looks like we're not even getting scanned to go in anymore.

We took the elevator down to the lower level and got out. We made a right and walked up a small ramp. We then entered a small hallway with giant portraits of Morgan Lewis, Daniel D. Tompkins and Jacob Morton. I told the two of them that they were premier Masons back in the day. We walked into what looked like a conference room by day, but at night there was quite a sight to see.

I counted 5 strippers, a DJ, and 5 men in suits. If we weren't in a Masonic lodge, you could never tell they were masons. Their usual garb wasn't on. One of them saw me and pointed.

"Well what do we have here?" the first man asked. "My name is Andrew. And who are you?"

I'm Pikachu," I said.

"I'm Sonic," Jackson said.

"I'm Bowsette," Larisa said.

"Who the hell is Bowsette?" the man asked.

"You know, Bowser and Peach had a baby. Bowsette," she said.

"Whatever, well welcome to my party!" He said enthusiastically as he humped Larisa. He turned back to everyone and went back to his seat after he had satisfied himself. He sat down and lit a cigar with a $100 bill. Everyone else lit their cigars.

"I trust that you brought what we asked for," Andrew said.

Jackson went to the cart and started pushing it towards him. Andrew eagerly opened up the cart and a billow of smoke came out. He wafted it away, which is literally all that dumbass guard had to do.

"Wow, you really went all out. I'm seriously impressed. Did we pay for all this?" Andrew asked as he turned, smacked a strippers ass and laughed.

"No baby, this one is special just for you," Larisa said as she pulled out a bottle of Louis XIII and handed it over to him.

"I've never seen one of these. Are you sure sweetcheeks?" he asked.

Larisa nodded.

"Larisa, I swear you did not buy a bottle of Louis XIII for this party on my card, did you?" Jean asked through the talkie.

"Relax," she whispered so only we could hear, "Someone I helped out a long time ago owed me a favor. I had a little sleeping magic added to it. It's not actually Louis XIII, it's just the bottle and basically Johnny Walker Blue," she said.

"Wait, you drugged them?" I asked. She had not revealed that part of the plan to us.

"Not drug, just suggestible," Larisa said and giggled.

"You bought a bottle of Johnny Blue for them?" Jean asked.

"Relax baby, I had to. Think of it as a necessary campaign expenditure," Larisa said.

"A toast to all my brothers in Masonry," Andrew said as he poured shots for everyone minus us.

"Cheers." They all said as they took the shot down.

"How long do we have to wait for this to kick in?" Jackson asked.

"Relax, either they're going to get hammered and pass out, or they're going to pass out," Larisa said.

My thoughts turned to the server room. Once we were done here, we were going to have to get past all the cameras that line the main hallway. The elevator we came down was not the same one that we were going to have to take up. Maybe that's why Larisa brought the balloons, to block us out. We were going to have to lose the costumes and hide behind them. My thoughts turned back to the door as our friendly security officer was staring at us.

"Are these people supposed to be here?" he asked.

"Of course, they are the party. We're fine here Ed. You can go back," Andrew said.

The man turned around confused and still a little dizzy from his second breath of life. Like Jackson said, he must have thought it was all a dream.

"I must say, I am incredibly turned on right now," Andrew began, "This is the best party I've had in a long time."

"Well, it's all for you so enjoy it," another man said.

"I thought these guys were not supposed to drink or do drugs," Jackson said.

"They're not supposed to when in a meeting or ritual. There's technically no rules against partying though," I said.

Just then I got another anonymous text message from the Internet:

In about 30 minutes there will be a shift change. Go then.

Josh was keeping tabs on us with this. It was comforting to know.

"Hey guys, just got a text. We've got half an hour and then 15 minutes to make this happen. Can we speed this up?" I asked.

"Roger that," Larisa said. Just like that she unzipped her costume and started sliding it down.

"What are you doing?!" I asked incredulously.

"Yeah, what is she doing?" Jean asked.

"She's taking her costume off," Jackson said.

"Relax guys, I'm leaving the head on," she said.

She took her costume off and was in her bra and panties.

"Well look who came to the party. Come here girl," Andrew said as the others looked on.

Larisa walked seductively and went to the Louis bottle. She moved the shot glasses out of the way and put a spout on top of the bottle.

"Open wide baby," she said.

She then took the bottle and poured a good 4 shots into his mouth. He swallowed it and smiled. She gave him a hug and rubbed her breasts on his face. She then stood up and started walking to each of the other men in the room who were preoccupied with the strippers that were there. She poured about 2-3 shots worth in each of their mouths and gave them the same treatment she gave Andrew. They all smiled and hollered. I don't think the strippers were too pleased that Larisa was stealing the show, but that's showbiz baby. She then guided their eyes to follow her ass back over to the balloons. Knowing what was in each she took a pen from the desk and popped 6 of the balloons. Out fell fuzzy handcuffs, finger traps, KY, flavored blowjob gel, everything you could imagine. She started tossing the handcuffs out to the strippers. At this point the medicine in the liquor was starting to work on them and they were getting dizzy.

"How did you get those in here, you naughty girl?" Andrew asked, slightly inebriated.

Larisa just put a finger to her costumes mouth and leaned forward as if to signal it was a secret. Then she shimmied.

Half an hour later and the strippers had half undressed the men and had them handcuffed. The concoction had started to work.

"I'm feeling woozy. Time to take this party home," Andrew said.

Larisa laughed silently into her earpiece and put her costume back on. It was a bit chilly in the lodge, I don't really know how she handled that being half naked.

"Who's coming home with me?" one of the men said. One stripper giggled.

We grabbed the balloons and we bowed and curtsied. Everyone whooped and hollered. They were still handcuffed to the chair, and Andrew was about to pass out. We turned to leave when we heard Andrew call us.

"We're keeping this liquor! We will definitely be calling you again," he said.

Larisa in order to save face, walked back up to him and gave him a hug. He took out a wad of hundreds and gave her a thousand dollars. She then turned and, still with the balloons in hand, we left and entered the elevator. I looked at my watch. It was time for the shift change. We were right on time.

We got out on the main floor and turned left and made another left to the other elevators. Larisa, careful to use the balloons to block the cameras, lead the way, and we went in the elevator. I pressed the 9th floor. We then all started taking our costumes off, leaving the heads on just in case. We left the costumes in the doorway of the elevator in order to keep it open until we got back. We turned the corner and there we saw it. The server room. The only problem was there was a thumbprint identification to get into the room. Larisa pulled a latex glove out of her pocket and put it on and put her thumb up to the screen. It beeped, turned green and then unlocked. She turned to us and did a little victory dance. I forgot that she had a master print. Once in the server room we got to work.

"Ok guys, so here's the server, we need to get in here," Larisa said.

The server was indeed protected by a Faraday cage, but that was mostly because the floor was carpet, and they didn't want static electricity getting in there. Either that or they really didn't want anyone trying to electrocute the server. God knows what kind of secrets are in this thing. There was a small lock on the cage, like one you would find on a diary. All this security and such a small lock? I thought.

"Alright guys look for the key," Larisa said.

We all spent about 3-4 minutes checking every draw, every potential hiding place to no avail.

"Jackson, can you just break this thing off?" I asked.

"Not without damaging the cage," he said.

We sat there stumped for a minute. Until Jackson noticed a can of compressed air on the shelf. He picked it up and gave it a small shake. It was full.

"Guys get out of the way," he said.

He took the air canister upside down and sprayed the lock. After about 20 seconds, the entire lock was frozen. He then took a paperweight from the desk and knocked the lock off.

"What the hell was that?" I asked.

"When you turn an air canister upside down it sprays 1,1,1-Trifluorethane which freezes metal. Gotta use what you have to make it work right bud?" he asked me through the earpiece.

We opened the Faraday cage and pulled the server out. Larisa did some quick work on it that I wasn't sure what she did. She put her terabyte flash drive in and backed the entire system up.

"How long?" I asked.

"About 5 minutes," she said.

"That leaves us 5 minutes to get the hell out of here.

Five long tense minutes went by, and finally she pulled the drive out.

"OK, I've got it. Wait one second," she said.

She walked over to the balloons that we tied to the door and popped one. Another flash drive fell out.

"Is that what I think it is?" I asked.

"Just get ready to run if we need to," she said.

She plugged the kill drive into the server.

"How long is this going to . . ." I said. Before I could say take, we saw an electrical discharge from it into the server. Suddenly the lights in the building went off and the emergency red lights came on. Larisa took the drive out, put the server back in the Faraday cage and zip tied it shut with a zip tie that was on the desk. She undid the balloons from the door, and we ran to the elevator. We got in and went down to the main floor. We ran out the front door to Jean in the van waiting for us. We got in and slammed the door, leaving the heads of our costumes on the street of 24th and 6th. Jean stepped on the gas as everything is a one way in New York City, he had to make a few turns to get back to the hotel. He shot a look over to Larisa like he was mad at her. She turned to him and gave him a kiss on the cheek and told him she loved him. That was the first time I had heard her say that to him, and his entire demeanor changed once he heard that. We had to hold up in our hotel so Larisa could comb through the information she just ripped. We had no idea what we just started.

I awoke only to find that the rest of the world was still asleep—Leonardo Da Vinci

Chapter Nine

"That's weird," Jean said.

"What's weird?" I asked.

"I could have sworn that unmarked cop car was following us. That was weird," he said.

"Let's just get back to the hotel," Larisa said.

We drove around for another half an hour to make sure that nobody was following us. Finally, we turned onto 24th Street and pulled into the parking garage. Jean turned the ignition off.

"I'm worried you're having too much fun with all of this," Jean said to Larisa.

"What do you mean?" she asked.

"These are extremely dangerous people that we're dealing with. I don't know why it always has to be on us to figure these things out, but I worry about you," he said pleading to her.

"Awww my mushball," Larisa said as she gave him a kiss "Don't worry about me. Jackson was with us the whole time. I'm sure he could have taken them out if we needed it," she said.

"Not dressed up as Sonic I couldn't," he said.

"Well whatever, let's just go inside so I can figure out what's on this hard drive," she said.

We got out of the car and made our way into the elevator. Took it to the top floor and got out. There were only two rooms on this floor. They were giant suites. Jean swiped his card to let us into one of the rooms.

We went inside and the first thing I noticed was that it was extremely well lit. I ran and shut the curtains.

"What's going on guys?" Hannah said, coming out of the bathroom wiping her mouth.

"Did you throw up again? What's with you sweetie?" I asked.

"I'm fine. Just got worried about you guys there," she said.

I never realized the anxiety I was putting her through with everything that we do. I walked up to her and gave her a bear hug. Larisa plugged the flash drive into her laptop and started typing away. Rosette was watching TV. Blur was back on again; I think this was a rerun. He was talking about how Apricot seeds, Vitamin B17 cure cancer. I turned the TV off.

"What did you do that for? I was starting to get into it," Rosette said.

"We need to figure out where we're going next," I said.

"That reminds me, I did pick something else up for all of us," Larisa said as she went into the back room where her bags must have been placed. She ran back out with a duffle bag and pulled out six grey sweatshirts and threw us each one of them.

"What is this for?" I asked.

"Who knows, it might save your life one day. Put it on," she said.

I didn't have time to argue with her, so I just put mine on. Sherpa, extremely comfortable.

"These are cozy," I said.

"Good, now listen what we're looking for," she started and paused as her eyes grew wide.

"He's back isn't he?" I asked.

She looked up and nodded.

What did you learn at the Masonic Lodge?

"Can you still hear us right now?" Larisa asked.

I can always hear you.

"Alright, well I'm looking into it right now. You'll have to give me a little bit," she said.

Alright, just ping me when you're done.

She shook her head and started typing away on the computer.

"This is incredible. There are donations, financials, little dossiers on each member of the Lodge as well as

Micah T. Dank

maintenance and everybody that comes in and out of it," she said.

"Hold on, it's not letting me access certain files. Let me kick the backdoor open and see what kind of coding is going on in this security," she said.

"Does anybody here know what that means?" I asked.

Silence.

"Alrighty then. Let us know when you have something," I said.

"So, Graham remember how I was telling you about Biocentrism?" Jackson said.

"Yes," I replied.

"Think about it like this in a way. Did you know that there are some forms of grass that produce DMT?" he asked.

I blinked.

"They do. Also, the smell of grass after it's cut, what every Hank Hill loving suburban New Balance wearing Dad with the grill tongs lives for? That's actually a distress signal from the grass. They communicate with each other. Grass does have a level of consciousness, and consciousness is fundamental," he said.

"That's actually pretty interesting. I know that if everything has a vibration then everything has a certain life quality to it. Also, isn't what you just described the plot of that movie The Happening? When the flowers and grass turn against humanity?" I asked.

"I've never seen it, but I'll take your word for it," Jackson said.

"OK, I've got something really weird here," Larisa said.

"What is it?" I asked.

"So, it all looks like generic coding but then I came across this section of code that has no functionality. In fact, it serves no purpose. It looks like it was literally planted into the encryption. Kind of like when you told me the story before I came around to the info on the DNA, this could be something," she said. "Or it could be complete crap and just there to confuse us."

"Well what does it say?" Rosette asked.

"It's not what it says, it doesn't say anything, it looks like it's binary," she replied.

"Show us," Jean said.

Larisa stood up and went over to the giant tv on the wall and turned the TV on. Blur was still talking about the Rife Machine. In 1934 Dr. Rife knew that everything vibrates at its own natural frequency. He believed that if he could figure out the frequencies of the disease causing viruses and bacteria, he could destroy them by matching the vibration frequency. Apparently, he used his machine to cure 16 patients with cancer before he was shut down.

Larisa turned it on AUX and plugged her computer into the HDMI component. The screen blinked then lit up. Here's what we saw.

01000110 01101111 01110101 01101110 01100100
00100000 01001001 01101110 00100000 01110100
01101000 01100101 00100000 01101100 01101111
01110011 01110100 00100000 01000001 01100011
01110100 01110011 00100000 01110111 01101000
01101001 01100011 01101000 00100000 01100100
01101001 01110011 01100011 01110101 01110011
01110011 01100101 01110011 00100000 01101001
01101110 01100110 01101001 01100100 01100101
01101100 01101001 01110100 01101001 01100101
01110011 00100000 01110100 01101000 01100101
00100000 01101100 01101001 01101011 01100101
01110011 00100000 01101111 01100110 00100000
01110111 01101000 01101001 01100011 01101000
00100000 01110111 01101111 01110101 01101100
01100100 00100000 01100100 01110010 01101001
01110110 01100101 00100000 01100001 00100000
01110010 01100101 01110110 01100101 01110010
01100101 01101110 01100100 00101100 00100000
01111010 01101111 01101111 01101101 00100000
01101001 01101110 00100000 01110100 01101111
00100000 01100001 00100000 01100011 01101001
01110110 01101001 01101100 00100000 01101001

01100011 01101111 01101110 00100000 01110011
01101000 01100001 01101101 01100101 01100100
00100000 01100110 01101111 01110010 00100000
01101001 01101110 01100110 01101001 01100100
01100101 01101100 01101001 01110100 01101001
01100101 01110011 00101110 00100000 01011001
01101111 01110101 00100000 01110111 01101001
01101100 01101100 00100000 01110011 01100101
01100101 00100000 01110100 01101000 01100101
00100000 01100011 01100101 01101110 01110100
01110010 01100001 01101100 00100000 01100010
01110101 01101001 01101100 01100100 01101001
01101110 01100111 00100000 01100110 01110101
01101100 01101100 00100000 01101111 01100110
00100000 01101100 01101001 01100001 01110010
01110011 00101100 00100000 01100011 01101000
01100101 01100001 01110100 01100101 01110010
01110011 00100000 01100001 01101110 01100100
00100000 01100011 01101111 01110101 01101110
01110100 01101100 01100101 01110011 01110011
00100000 01101001 01101110 01100110 01101001
01100100 01100101 01101100 01101001 01110100
01101001 01100101 01110011 00101110 00100000
01000110 01101111 01101100 01101100 01101111
01110111 00100000 01110100 01101000 01100101
00100000 01001110 01101111 01110010 01110100

01101000 00100000 00001101 00001010 01010011
01110100 01100001 01110010 00100000 01110111
01101000 01101001 01100011 01101000 00100000
01110111 01101001 01101100 01101100 00100000
01101100 01100101 01100001 01100100 00100000
01111001 01101111 01110101 00100000 01110100
01101111 00100000 01110100 01101000 01100101
00100000 01100110 01101111 01110101 01110010
00100000 01001000 01100101 01101100 01101001
01101111 00100000 01001000 01101111 01110010
01110011 01100101 01101101 01100101 01101110
00101110 00100000 01000010 01100101 01101110
01100101 01100001 01110100 01101000 00100000
01110100 01101000 01100101 00100000 01100011
01100001 01110010 01110010 01101001 01100001
01100111 01100101 00100000 01101001 01110011
00100000 01110111 01101000 01100001 01110100
00100000 01111001 01101111 01110101 00100000
01110011 01100101 01100101 01101011

"Well, what do you think it is?" I asked.

"Could it be Morse code?" Jean asked.

"We've been through that once before, but I'll check," I said.

I searched on the internet for any logical meaning behind this sequence of numbers. Nothing came up. I was starting to get frustrated when Hannah came up behind me and gave me a hug and humped me from the back. I don't know who you are if you're not with someone that does that to you. I smiled. Then I had an idea.

"What if it's location points? What if we add the numbers up. Is that significant?" I asked.

"Hmmmmm, I don't think so. Nothing special with the number and I don't know any location that has this many numbers in its location.

"Could it be different latitude and longitudes?" I asked. Funny I should say that.

"No that's not it either," Rosette said.

"Guys I'm getting hungry. I'm ordering room service," Hannah said.

I turned to her, what is it with this girl lately, she's been acting funny.

"Wait. I think I know what it is!" Larisa exclaimed.

"What would that be?" Jean asked.

"I think it's Binary," Larisa said.

"We know it's Binary," Jean said.

"You didn't let me finish Jean. What I meant was I think it's Binary for language. This translates to a language, I believe," she said as she started typing away.

We waited for a few minutes as her computer did the work. Suddenly she sat back and a look of shock came on her face. Shock and excitement. I think Jean is right, she really is into this.

Found In the lost Acts which discusses infidelities the likes of which would drive a reverend, zoom in to a civil icon shamed for infidelities. You will see the central building full of liars, cheaters and countless infidelities. Follow the North Star which will lead you to the four Helio Horsemen. Beneath the carriage is what you seek

"Any ideas?" Jean asked.

"The only lost Acts I know about are from Paul. It's an apocryphic text that was said to be lost in time. Supposedly there is a rumor that the Library of Alexandria held the entire Apocrypha collection. I have no idea if it discussed infidelities though. I assume it might have," I said.

"What are you two doing Larisa?" Jean asked.

"I'm just having a glass of Rose with Rose, my partner in wine," she said as she winked to Rosette. Rosette giggled.

"So, found in Paul then?" Jackson asked.

"Maybe St. Paul?" Hannah injected.

We looked over to her. I nodded my head.

"A civil icon shamed for infidelities would be MLK, right?" Larisa asked as she pounded a gulp of pink wine.

"But zooming into MLK? What could that mean?" Jean asked.

"Everything is named Martin Luther King something or other, isn't it?" I asked.

"Exactly," Jackson said.

"Larisa, can you look up a Martin Luther something or other in St. Paul?" I asked.

Larisa started typing furiously.

"Well there's a MLK Rec Center in St. Paul," she said.

"I doubt anything has to do with a Rec Center," I said.

Rosette pounded her glass and poured herself another one and turned back on the TV.

Halliburton can't build the FEMA camps fast enough to keep us all in line, you second dimensional bastards! AHHHHHH! Sorry, I didn't mean to snap there, but I just can't stand the globalists. I know this is a good Christian fanbase here.

"Damn it, Rosette," I said as I grabbed the remote and turned it off. "We're in the middle of something."

"I know, but he's just so addictive, isn't he?" she said.

"What other location would MLK have in St. Paul? Come on Larisa," I said.

"Slow down muchacho. There's a Martin Luther King Jr Boulevard as well," she said.

"Is there anything on it?" I asked.

"The state capitol building is on it actually," she said.

"The likes of which would drive a reverend. 75 Rev Dr Martin Luther King Jr Boulevard," I said.

"The central building full of liars, cheaters and countless infidelities. Sounds like a politician's den to me," Jean said.

"Minnesota's motto is that it is the "Star of the North. The North Star. This is it guys," I said.

"But what about the Helio Horsemen?" Rosette asked.

"Christ represents the Sun. The Sun dies in Sagittarius. Sagittarius is the man on the horse. There are four gospels in the canon. Each horseman kills the Sun. That's how we get the four horsemen," I said.

"I think we've heard that from you before. Maybe I read it somewhere," Jackson said.

"The four Suns dying in Sagittarius. There has to be an apocryphal clue at the capitol building in St. Paul. Jean, how do you want to handle this?" I turned and asked him. Though we were using one of his family's planes, I didn't want to just go and assume.

"This is perfect. I'll have it gassed up and ready to go in two hours," he said as he took out his phone and made a call.

"Um your plane is in Boston. We're still in New York Jean," Jackson said.

"Merde," Jean said. "Alright make it a few more hours. Actually, I need to run out for a little bit," he said as he turned to the other room.

I went into the back room and started bringing out everybody's suitcases. We had a few hours to burn, but I wanted to make sure that we were ready to go when he was. I had no idea what we were looking for when we got to Minnesota. Truthfully, I wish we hadn't gone. I had already lost one of my best friends to some dangerous activity. I had been tortured beyond belief. Nothing compares to the torture I would endure, as well as losing each and every one of them. I was going to need a miracle.

A fool thinks he knows everything and is content in his own ignorance. A wise man seeks knowledge from the cradle to the grave and still recognizes he knows nothing—Anonymous

Chapter Ten

We waited for Jean to come back, and when he finally did two hours later, he had a giant duffle bag with him. None of us had any idea why, but we had to run to catch a flight. So we loaded up everything and got into the van and made our way back to Boston. Things were a little tight with this big duffle bag in the car, but we made it work.

"Hey Jean, what did you go out and buy?" I asked.

"A prototype I've always wanted. Remember when I told you earlier that I bought a new toy?" he asked.

"Well, what kind of prototype?" Rosette asked.

"It's an aviation jetpack," he said as he turned and smiled at us from the driver's seat.

There was silence.

"Jean, let me ask you a question. You were mad at me when you thought I bought a bottle of Louis XIII and then you go out and buy a flying machine?" Larisa asked.

"I'm sorry I got on your case about the Louis XIII. But I had been waiting for this for a while. They opened a flagship store in the city, and instead of having this shipped, I just went to pick mine up. Number 5 out of 100 made so far," he said and grinned.

Larisa rolled her eyes and went to work on her laptop when she got a message.

Where are you all headed?

"Minnesota," she said.

"What?" I asked.

"He's back," she said. We all nodded.

What's in Minnesota?

"A clue. Something about four Horsemen and the State Capitol Building. They said that there would be a clue by the North Star," she said.

The man who controls the balance was silent for a moment. Then he started typing again.

Have you looked at the Capitol Building yet?

"No, but I will now," Larisa said as she started typing away at her computer. After a few minutes she stopped typing.

"Hey guys," she started. "The giant star is in the middle of the building. There's nothing near it, but there is a monument on the top of the building. Four golden Horsemen and a carriage. This must be it. This has to be the clue," she said.

The man never responded. I was beginning to wonder if he was just leading us so we could do his dirty work for him. I wasn't about to argue with someone who could hear us no matter where we were. I did not want to test this.

"Guys, I'm trying to pull up the floor plan for this building, but I don't see a way up there. Jean, it looks like we're going to have to get some rope and climb it like Jackson did in Arizona, so I heard," she said.

"Wait, can't we just use Jean's new equipment instead?" Hannah asked.

"Jean?" Larisa asked.

"Let's see what it's like when we get there, it's going to be a lot more inconspicuous if we climb the building instead of, you know, flying through town," he said.

We agreed. We sat there and started discussing what our next point of attack would be. I started rethinking my position on the man. He just asked a question, he didn't exactly lead us there or maybe he did. I couldn't be sure if he knew what was going on, and he just wanted us to go through the motions that seems like a very lazy thing to do.

We made the few hour trip back to Boston, it had started raining a bit, so it took us longer than expected. We took the van directly to private parking at the airport and got out with our bags and made our way to the runway. The plane was sitting there, open and inviting. I swear we were getting spoiled at this point. I didn't know if we could fly coach anymore. I never thought I'd say that, but I understand why these millionaire preachers with their own jets tell people they HAVE to have them. The preaching machines, or so they called them.

We got on the plane, it was going to be a three-and-a-half-hour flight due to the weather. We saddled up and Jackson helped Jean lug this giant machine with him. I began thinking that if Jean didn't want it used, then he would have left it in the Van in parking. Or maybe he thought that someone would steal it. I mean he did just drop six figures on this thing.

The flight was a boring old flight. We talked about nonsense mostly. Mostly about how the Masonic Lodge ended up working out and how ridiculous people can be. We did however make the news. Blur was on the TV in the main room talking about how someone broke into the Masonic Lodge in New York City and blew out the server. He called it a great win against the New World Order and suggested that this would happen many more times before this was all said and done. I laughed and changed the channel to the weather trying to figure out if this rain was ever going to stop. It seemed to be following us to the Midwest.

We got to MSP airport and Jean had a giant Escalade waiting for us with an extended rear. You could fit nine people in this thing. Little did we know that I would soon need to have room for 7 people permanently but not before everyone in this plane was taken away from me.

The worst pain a man can suffer is to have insight into much and power over nothing—Herodotus

Chapter Eleven

We got into the ginormous car and Jean punched the coordinates into his phone instead of the cars nav system. Didn't want to leave any record of where we were going which, knowing our luck in the past, was a smart thing. We went directly to our hotel which was only a few miles away from the Capitol Building. We had to wait until dark.

We sat around our hotel room for a few hours just talking. So far nothing had gotten too crazy. Famous last words, right? I know. Still though, we were talking about how blessed we were that we were all still here and able to save the world again so to speak. Although I'm not really sure if we're actually saving anything or destroying things. My appearances and books have been so controversial that I've apparently now gotten TMZ involved in my life. I guess I didn't realize how big I was becoming. It's amazing that I can still be pretty incognito at this point. If things do get any worse, I'll shave my head and grow a beard out and stop doing talks and lectures.

We didn't bother bringing the suitcases or Jean's machine into the hotel room. We figured we'd get it later. We made our way to the Capitol Building. It was actually beautiful once we got there and looked at it. It was lit up purple for some reason and the glow was just amazing. We looked up to the roof and saw the chariot and horsemen. The golden piece, offset by the purple was pretty cool, not going to lie. We looked around and there seemed to be nobody there. No security, no people around it. This was going to be the time we were going to have to make it happen.

"Jean, how loud is your thing? Also how do you use it?" I asked.

"I don't know how loud it is, and it's gassed and ready to go. It's like a joystick for a video game. You press the button, it gasses it, and you float up," he said.

"Are you sure you want to use this now?" Rosette asked.

"Look around. This is the clearest shot we're going to get. Alright fine. I'll try and get in the Capitol Building the old fashioned way," I said as I made my way up to the entrance. The doors were locked. Typical.

"Do you want to pick this Rosette, or can I just go up there?" I asked.

"Alright fine I'll pull it out. I wanted to be the first person to use this to be honest with you, but I won't hold it against you," Jean said.

It took him a few minutes, but he and Jackson pulled it out of the car, unzipped the bag and set it up.

"Alright so you wear it as a backpack and use the controller like I mentioned. Don't pull your feet all the way back or the jets will burn your legs off," Jean said.

"These shoot flames?" I asked.

"No, but they do generate heat from burning fuel," Jean said.

"Have you ever seen anyone actually do this before?" I asked.

"One time, at the demonstration. I was sold on it from the beginning," he said.

I put the machine on and then took it off.

"Hey Jax, you're closer, can you grab my hoodie that Larisa gave us, it's in the car?" I asked.

"Sure thing, no problem buddy," he said.

He walked over to the car and grabbed the hoodie and tossed it to me.

"Alright I'm ready, wish me luck," I said as I turned the jets on.

I pressed the buttons and started to float up. You know that feeling when you're on the pirate's ship at an amusement park, the one where it goes back and forth super high and you feel weightless and that aerodynamic feeling in your balls, well I just got that with this thing. This thing was awesome. There's just no other word to capture it. I started going up slow at first, but eventually I went up a little faster until I had enough balls to really shoot up to the top. I went about 10 feet above it and slowly released the buttons, and it let me fall slowly until I landed on the floor next to it. These things weren't loud at all and super fun. I had no idea how much fuel I had left, so I didn't waste much time. I went under the carriage as advised, and I felt a keypad and a scroll right next to it. I grabbed the scroll and tore it off and went back to the jetpack.

"Alright guys, I'm coming back down," I said.

"Roger that," Jackson said.

I saw that there were people starting to walk around our general area, so I decided to let myself down through the back of the building and walk around. Went through the same motions as I did to lower myself down to the main level when I overshot it, and, after a minute or two, I was back down on the ground. I took the Jetpack off and walked up to the car and placed it in the backseat.

"Hey guys, you have to try," I began as I turned around and froze in horror. There was a man with a baretta aimed right at my friends and wife.

"Don't move a muscle kid," the man said.

"Wait, we can talk about this," I said.

"There's nothing to talk about. Did you think that what happened in New York was going to stay in New York?" he asked.

I didn't say anything.

"Around here, in these parts we don't mess around. No rituals, no religious clues, nothing. Just an end of the line for you," he said.

I tried to scream and no sound came out. I just froze as I watched him shoot each of them one by one in the midsection. I couldn't see from where I was if it was the heart, but they all fell and did not move. They lay there for a minute completely still and not breathing.

"Give me the keys," the man said as he came over to me.

I stared blankly at him.

He reloaded his gun.

I absentmindedly tossed him the keys. He then walked around and started the car, came back to me, still frozen staring at my wife, dead on the floor and smacked me in the face with the butt of the gun. That's the last thing I remember before everything went black.

When you go through that spiritual awakening, nothing bothers you anymore. Because nothing matters. You realize you're just a passenger on this earth with a limited time. Your mission here is to observe and learn. And then you go back far away from here—Jim Carrey

Chapter Twelve

I woke up in a small room that I had never seen before. My head was pounding. I stood up and looked around, holding my head in my hands. Then everything all came flooding back. The man that did this to me had taken away everyone that meant anything to me. I felt defeated, deflated. I no longer cared about my well-being or my self-preservation. I wanted out of this miserable existence. My head started spinning. What if I had deleted that email? What if I stayed in Med school? What if Hannah and I had moved far away from all that had become of my life in the last few years. I sat down and started to weep. I lifted my head up long enough to see something that startled me in the corner.

There was a mannequin dressed similar to me surrounded by 12 stone birds. It appeared to be some kind of ritual. And then all at once it hit me. The silence.

I could hear my heart beating. I also heard what sounded like running water going through my ears but couldn't place it. Was I in a bunker under water? I never would have guessed until I heard the voice.

"Hello Graham," the voice said over speaker.

"Where am I?" I asked.

"Don't worry about where you are. Just know that you're not getting out of here alive, unless you give me what I want," he said.

"What is that exactly?" I asked.

"The scroll that you captured. We oversaw those that were keeping this secret as we have been for eons. I can't believe that it's you out of all people that found it, but then again I shouldn't be surprised. This is what you do for a living isn't it?" the voice continued.

"Who are you?" I asked.

"You can call me Sir Ciao," he said snickering.

"Ciao, as in goodbye in Italian? You know," I said as I started to stand up despite the enormous pain in my head. I could feel the heartbeat in my temples and my frontal cortex was throbbing. "I don't suppose you have any aspirin or vicodin back there, do you?" I said.

"I admire you Mr. Newsdon. Clearly the fact that all your friends and family are dead hasn't taken away your wiseass attitude that I've grown to love in your books," Sir said.

"Am I supposed to honestly call you Sir?" I asked.

"What you call me doesn't matter. But if I'm willing to do that to those you love, there's still people that I can come after. Your friends in the Rosicrucians. Those pesky people at Senna Ore. Those cousins of yours that you don't talk to anymore. I can make it so that anybody that's ever been connected to you disappears into the ocean, unless you give me that scroll. I checked your pockets and shoes while you were knocked out, and I couldn't find it. Where is it?" Sir asked.

"You're going to feel really let down," I began, "but I don't have it with me," I said.

Sir was silent for two minutes. Two long agonizing minutes. What was that noise I couldn't figure out. It was driving me crazy.

"People are not supposed to be in this room for more than 45 minutes without a guide. You hear that noise in your ears Graham. Sounds like running water. That's your blood flowing through your body. You're in the quietest room on planet Earth. It's actually negative decibels in there. You're at Orfield Labs in Minneapolis. It's ironic that you're so close to the Capitol, yet nobody will ever find you. It's a Saturday and this place is closed. You will have lost your mind permanently by the time this place reopens on Monday," he said.

"What's with the mannequin?" I asked.

"Don't worry about that. Consider him your last friend and that being a final message to you to not mess with us. Now, where did you leave the scroll. Did you hide it in the car?" Sir asked.

Again, I was silent.

"Alright, you want to play that game, we can play that game. See you in half an hour," he said.

He stopped communication, and I was left there with my thoughts, which in this room sounded like someone was shouting at me through my head. My headache was starting to go away a bit. After a few minutes of dead silence, I started to become uncomfortable. A few minutes after that I started to panic a bit, so I started talking to myself to hear a voice, any noise besides my stomach, my blood and my heart. I then decided I would start talking to the Mannequin. I crawled over to him. He was very lifelike. I tried to figure out what this symbolized, or if I had anything in my arsenal that could explain it, but I was drawing a blank. I slithered back to the section I was sitting in. Another 15 minutes went by and I was starting to lose my mind. Until finally I heard the voice again.

"Congratulations Graham, you've just survived your first thirty minutes in there. Can you imagine doing this for the next 24 hours?" Sir asked.

"You can do what you want to me, but I'm not going to tell you where the scroll is," I said.

I could hear the instant rage that bubbled up inside of Sir. Within two minutes I heard a locking mechanism and the door open. He was back with a gun.

He did not look anything like what I expected. He was about my height, very fit and had two giant tattoos on his forearms. One was an "I" and one was an "S". And he was aiming a gun directly at my head.

"Take your clothes off Graham," he said.

"This is really not putting me in the mood," I said.

He smiled and came up to me and slapped me across the face.

"I'm not screwing around with you boy. I will kill you in here just like your wife and friends. Start stripping," he said.

Reluctantly I started taking my clothes off. I should have not done it. I should have made him shoot me. My mother and father and brother were all dead. My friends and my wife were dead. What's the point? Yet, self-preservation is still a thing that is very much a part of all of us here on this Planet. I got down to my boxers. Sir picked up my clothes and combed through every single inch of it but found nothing.

"Take your boxers off," he said.

I took my boxers off. There I stood completely naked in front of the man who was surely going to kill me, and he was about to finger my asshole looking for a scroll. I should have planned for this. I should have come up with a better hiding spot.

"If I find a scroll in there, you're dead for making me do this," Sir said as he snapped on a rubber glove. "Squat."

I did as instructed and squatted. He shoved his finger up my ass. My butt clenched up once he did that, and he punched me in the leg. I loosened it as best I could. Finally, after finding nothing, he threw the glove in the corner and furiously stood up.

"Fine, another hour of this then. We've got all the time in the world Graham," Sir said as he slammed the door.

The next hour he didn't talk, didn't say a word, nothing. It was just me and my thoughts, my body sounds and my throbbing asshole. He was never going to find the scroll, but he needed me alive to tell him where it was, after that I was expendable. I knew I wasn't going to be able to make it past 2 hours let alone 24 hours of this silent torture.

After an hour, I heard the door start to open. My mindset was not there. Mind you, nobody has ever stayed in this room longer than 45 minutes, let alone without someone else. I started hearing a voice in my head talking back to me.

Just end your life already. You'll never get out of here alive to begin with.

Shut up! I said to myself.

Who would miss you anyway if you left?

Again, shut up!

I argued with myself for that moment, before the door opened up, and I saw Sir Ciao again. He looked at me and started shaking his head. Then he made his way over to where I was and sat down on the floor, tapping his gun on the floor.

"Graham, come on. How much more of this do you want to endure?" he asked.

"I have nothing to live for anymore. But I will never give the scroll up to you," I said to him.

He looked over to me and smiled. "The voices have started, haven't they?" he asked and laughed.

I stared blankly at him.

"I wouldn't be surprised if they never went away at this point. You've been broken my friend. Just end this pain for yourself," he said to me.

I looked over at him, and with the last bit of strength I had I spit in his face.

He looked at me bewildered and wiped the spit from his face. "If that's how you want it," he said as he raised his gun towards my chest and fired a round into my heart.

All things are possible. Who you are is limited by who you think you are—Egyptian Book of the Dead

Chapter Thirteen

I hit the ground with a pain that I can only compare to when Marshall shot me in Israel. I couldn't breathe, couldn't move, couldn't feel. And then all at once it occurred to me. Why am I still alive after a point blank shot? Sir stood up and walked over to my body and looked at me gasping for air.

"You're still alive?" he asked bewildered.

Just as soon as he got the word alive out, I heard another crack of a gun and saw Sir stunned. He dropped his gun and fell to his knees. Then I heard another shot and saw the left side of his head blown off and splatter all over me and the mannequin. I managed to open my eyes past the squint that I had been looking at him and saw who it was.

It was Josh, my old friend. The Mason somehow, someway found me. I was overwhelmed with emotion. He walked over to me and helped me to my feet.

"We don't have much time, we have to get the hell out of this anechoic chamber," he said to me.

I just looked at him and wrapped my arms around him tightly and squeezed. I had not lost everybody, and I had just survived the closest encounter to death since I was in the white room. I was beginning to wonder if there was any permanent brain damage going on with me at this point.

"Where are we going?" I finally got out through labored breaths, clutching my chest.

"We're going to the hotel. There're some people that are going to be very happy to see you. We're just waiting for Rosette and Hannah to get back from the hospital," he said as his eyes dropped to the mannequin and the stone birds surrounding them.

"Wait, they're alive?" I asked.

"Hold on a sec Graham," he said.

He looked at it for a few minutes and finally holstered his gun. What he said next stunned me.

"And having made soft clay, he fashioned thereof twelve sparrows. And it was the Sabbath when he did these things. And there were also many other little children playing with him. And Joseph came to the place and saw; and cried out to him, saying: Wherefore doest thou these things on the Sabbath, which it is not lawful to do? But Jesus clapped his hands together and cried out to the sparrows and said to them: Go! And the sparrows took their flight and went away chirping," he said.

"I'm not familiar with that," I said.

"Well you better start learning it. That's from the Infancy Gospel of Thomas, it's a Gnostic text. Supposedly there is a secret society that's so ancient and powerful that they supersede all other societies. They don't talk in the canonized verses, they deal with the Gnostic texts, lost texts and books that have been removed from the Bible. If that's who this is, then this is only the beginning," he said.

I tried to change the subject. "How am I still alive?" I asked.

"Yeah. It turns out those sweatshirts that Larisa gave you all were called Wonder Hoodie's. They're bulletproof?" he asked.

I did wonder, but it didn't occur to me. It was so good to see colors, but the sounds of everyday were starting to get to me. It's how I imagined if a deaf person gained hearing, how they would feel until they acclimated.

"Wait, why were they at the hospital?" I asked.

Josh stopped walking and turned to me. "I'm sorry my friend, but that shot to your wife's stomach caused a miscarriage. There was nothing they could do," he said as he gave me a hug.

"She, she was pregnant?!" I asked bewildered as I fell to my knees and the most interesting wave of emotions ran over me. It was a combination of being at a tremendous loss for the baby that we made, but such gratefulness that they were all alive. I sat there for a moment, Josh letting me collect my thoughts when suddenly I felt a rage in me.

"Just out of curiosity, where did you stash the scroll?" he asked.

I turned to him. "How do you know so much about this?" I asked.

"Graham," he began as he looked me dead in the eyes. "I was a Mason. I knew certain things. They found out what I did with you and they kicked me out. They're probably on their way here to kill us. We don't have a lot of time. We'll be safe once we get to the hotel. Where is it?" he asked.

I lead him back into the room I was just in, stepping over Sir and walked over to the mannequin. I opened its mouth and pulled the scroll still encased in a thin plastic bottle. Sir didn't see, but when I went over to the mannequin earlier, I had stashed it there. You never see what's directly in front of your eyes.

"That's genius Graham. But why is it brown?" he asked.

"It was in my ass prior to this. I guess you could say I went ass to mouth," I said as I laughed and clutched my ribs, still extremely sore.

"Alright, let's get out of here," he said.

We got into his car and made our way to the hotel which was just a short ride away. We walked down that hallway, my palms sweaty the entire time. I wasn't going to believe they were still alive until I saw them. Finally, we got to the door and Josh used the keycard that one of them must have given him and opened the door.

They were all there looking at me with huge puppy dog eyes. I lost my mind. I started balling out crying. I walked into the middle of all of them and just gave them a big hug. Then I walked over to the bed where Hannah was lying, still in obvious pain and lay on her chest and cried. When I said earlier that I was willing to die for my beliefs and that I didn't care what happened to me, it never occurred to me that it could happen to those who were so close to me and THAT, as it turns out is so much worse.

"Alright guys. We need to roll out of here, but first, we need to figure out where we're going," Josh said.

"No way man, I'm done," Jackson said.

"We can't possibly keep this up," Larisa said.

"OK guys, first of all, kudos to Larisa for the bullet-proof attire. I suggest you keep wearing it, because wherever you go at this point, they know who you are and what you're up to. The only thing they don't have is the clue. We really need to figure this out and get going, at the very least, the hell out of Minnesota," Josh said.

We all looked at each other and agreed that we did need to leave and that we should have to figure out where we're going.

"If I wasn't all in before, I'm definitely in now. I feel like I'm back to life," I said.

"This is a suicide mission. Save yourself the time Graham."

"What did you just say?" I asked.

Josh looked over to me "Nobody said anything bud. You feeling ok?" he asked.

I'm still hearing voices. I don't know how I'm going to be able to function with that going on.

"Graham, what does the scroll say?" Jackson said, breaking up my inner monologue.

I grabbed the scroll and took it out of the plastic case, got up went to the bathroom and washed my hands and flushed the case down the toilet. Then I came back out and sat down and read it to them.

25183233. In the secret house of Khnum is a celestial sign that no longer holds true and has been lost within the ages. Locate the difference and seek out Boriska's secret.

"Anybody have a clue as to what that is?" Larisa asked.

"Not a clue. Is that a phone number or an address like the last clue?" I asked.

You're going to end up getting all your friends killed for real this time.

"Dammit!" I said as I pounded my fist on the table.

Everybody looked at me. I can't explain how strange this is. You have your own inner voice, the voice of your thoughts, and then it's like a completely different voice saying things to you. I was hoping that a good night's sleep would be able to shake this off, I was going to have to wait and see.

"Wait, did the scroll say Khnum?" I asked, trying to change the subject.

"You read it," Josh said.

"OK, let me just, let me just sit and think for a minute." I sat down and put my head in my hands this time, then a short while later came up.

"OK, so Khnum is an ancient Egyptian God. He had a human body and the head of a Ram. We know the Egyptians were around in Aries, but they were not the people of Aries. So, what's with this secret house? Hey Rosette, can you look to see if there are any secret palaces, or museums, or anything with Khnum?" I asked.

"Sure thing cap," she said as she smiled all giddy. Ever since Larisa came on board, there was less for her to do computerwise, but she was thrilled that I asked her to go back to her old searching ways.

"Graham, are you feeling ok?" Jackson asked.

"Yeah, why do you ask?" I asked.

"Because you keep looking around every few seconds. Did that soundproof place mess with you head or something?" he asked.

I wanted to tell them that I was slowly losing my mind. I wanted to tell them that I was hearing voices. That I wanted to commit myself to figure out what was going on with me because I knew it was not normal. But we were too far into this at this point. That was going to have to wait. I was just going to have to pray that I could keep it under control.

"Got something," Rosette said.

"What is it?" I asked.

"There's a Temple of Khnum in Egypt. This has to be it," she said.

"What makes you say that?" I asked.

"Because, there is an entire Zodiac drawn onto the ceiling of the Portico. The clue said to find the anomaly," she said. "Also, because that string of numbers provided are longitude and latitude coordinates. They show Esna," she finished.

She was right. This had to be it.

"I know where that is. It's basically in the middle of nowhere," Josh said.

"How do we get there?" Hannah asked.

I turned and looked at my wife. Everything that we've been through together, but nothing like what we just went through.

You lost your child with her. It's your fault that she had the miscarriage. If you had just said no to this rabbit hole, you could be home right now picking out furniture and baby names.

I slammed my hand down on the table. Everybody stopped and looked at me after I did that. I excused myself into the bathroom where I micro dosed again. That usually made me feel better. I'm not sure how long I'm going to be able to keep this façade up. I walked back into the room.

"Sorry about that, it's just been a rough 24 hours. So, how do we get there?" I asked.

"We're taking the plane to Cairo. Whoever found us obviously is plugged into us somehow, and we need to get off the grid. Once we're in Cairo we're going to take a train there. It should keep us off the grid," Josh said.

"How long of a trip is it?" Larisa asked.

"It's about 10.5 hours," Josh said.

"That's a crazy long time. So much can go wrong. Can't we fly directly into Esna?" Hannah asked.

"If we do that, we risk being known. Flight plans would be out there, plus they don't usually get so much traffic there. We'd stand out. No, it's best we fly to Cairo," Josh said.

"Alright, if you say so," I said.

"I'll make arrangements," Jean said as he took his phone out and went into the bathroom.

"Baby, are you sure you're ok?" Hannah asked as she came over to me and lay in my lap.

"After what you've been through, you're asking me if I'm OK when I'm just worried to death about you?" I asked.

She looked up at me and brought her face up to me and gave me a kiss.

"What happened back there was not your fault. No matter how much you think it was, do not blame yourself," she said.

I don't know if it was what she just said, or the fact that my mini dose was kicking in, but I felt better than I had in the last 48 hours. I was going to try to ride this wave of happiness out.

"Alright guys, we're ready to go. By the time we get to the airport it will be fueled and ready to go. Come on everybody, pack your stuff and let's get in the car," Jean said.

"Fine by me," I said as I got up and started collecting bags.

We were going to fly to Egypt again, a place I didn't think I was going to have to revisit since our last trip there. I was a little nervous about what was to come, but I figured if we survived this, then we could survive anything. Only this time we're all bringing the bullet-proof hoodies with us. A little added protection never hurt. I looked over the room and saw all my friends and realized how lucky and blessed I was to have them. I don't think until I thought they were all dead, that I truly appreciated them.

We got in Josh's car and made our way to the airport. I was relaxing in the back trying to get a few seconds of shut eye when I heard the voice clear as day, coming from within my head, in a very distinct voice.

You're all going to die tomorrow.

I opened my eyes. This was going to be a problem.

Against a stupidity that is in fashion, no wisdom compensates. Talk sense to a fool and he calls you foolish! Truth will always be truth, regardless of a lack of understanding, disbelief or ignorance—Sun of Saturn

Chapter Fourteen

We were halfway across the Atlantic when I woke up. Rosette as typical was deep into her Xanax cocktail, talking with Larisa about how scissoring works. I swear, these two are not good news together. I turned and looked to my side and saw Josh typing away on his computer.

"What are you doing buddy?" I asked.

"Oh, hey Graham. Have a nice nap? Naw, nothing much, just trying to research who would be using these gnostic text references," he said.

"Josh, do you know that the United States is basically the Roman Empire part two?" I began.

He stopped typing and looked at me.

"Caesar ruled from a place called Capitoline Hill in Rome. In the US they rule from Capitol Hill. Capitol Hill is in Washington DC, which is one of three epicenters of ruling. The Military rules from DC, the finance is in the City of London and spirituality is ruled from Vatican

City. They made sure to let you know about it though. There's a reason DC is directly between Virginia and Maryland. Or Virgin Mary," I said.

"If you only knew half the things I know Graham," he said as he turned back to the computer.

I closed my eyes for a second.

If this plane crashes, you will have died for nothing and the secret stays locked up forever.

I opened my eyes to see Jean, Hannah and Rosette sitting next to me.

"How did you survive the silent room?" he asked.

"I have no idea buddy, but I'm having some residual side effects," I said.

"What kind of side effects Newsdon," Rosette asked.

"Ah, never mind, I'm fine," I said.

"Baby, if you're going through something, we can help you out with it, you know that right?" Hannah asked.

I turned to her, leaned over and gave her a kiss. I still was rolling the idea in my head that I almost lost all of them not 24 hours ago.

"Newsdon, if you want to talk, let me know. Believe me, nobody has ever gone through what you just went through. Solitary confinement isn't even that cruel," Rosette said.

"I appreciate it Rose, but really, I'll be fine. I'm a pretty big bad ass actually. I've been to Facebook jail before. Also, I just did Ancestry and found out I'm a quarter Italian, so I'm built for this kind of stuff," I said.

"I've always wanted to try Ancestry. How does it work?" Jean asked.

"Well Jean," I said turning to him, "first they send you a tube, you drop a sample, then you mail it back in. Then in 6 weeks they give you the results," I said.

"What kind of sample?" he asked.

"You have to cum in the tube and seal it up real quickly," I said holding back my laughter.

"That's NOT how this works, don't listen to him Jean," Hannah said laughing.

"You're a sick bastard you know that Newsdon. Oooh, I wish you actually did that though. I would have loved to see how they responded," Rosette said.

I smiled and turned my head away and closed my eyes. I was trying to gain my strength back. Truthfully, when I'm asleep or about to fall asleep is the only time I have peace of mind. This voice in my head is exhausting.

I awoke sharply to our descent into Cairo. We landed at the airport and went through customs. Jean left the jet pack on the plane, so we didn't have to explain that. I was just hoping we weren't going to have to use it.

We all followed the signs to the train and Jean bought us each a ticket to Esna. We rolled our suitcases to the train terminal. After about a half an hour a train arrived, and we boarded. Not quite the TGV in France, but roomy and comfortable. I was looking around to see if they had a bar car. Hannah must have sensed what I was doing and made me sit down.

We talked for an hour or two until everyone started getting sleepy. Everybody said goodnight and within 20 minutes they were all passed out. I was left alone with my thoughts as I was wide awake.

Josh can't be trusted. You're too trusting in people. He's going to turn on you all as soon as you give him what he wants. Once a Mason always a Mason.

I closed my eyes hoping to make the voice go away. I tried everything. Tried depressing my breathing, tried meditating, nothing worked. It was going to be us two together until I fell asleep again, or until someone else woke up. I was in mental agony. I couldn't turn around now though. I had no idea what the next 24 hours was going to entail for me.

There are two ways to be fooled. One is to believe what isn't true, the other is to refuse to accept what is true—Kierkegaard

Chapter Fifteen

We got to Esna and I woke everybody up. Because I had slept on the plane, I hadn't slept during this train ride. I was exhausted but couldn't sleep. Whenever I'm exhausted, the voice gets worse and so does my depression. I still haven't dealt with my mother's death and nobody knew that I was hearing things. Keeping that from my friends was killing me, but unfortunately for me I had to keep slushing on.

We got off the train and hailed a cab. It was more like a Scooby Doo mystery van. One of those vans with only the back bubble window. The hooker vans they have in France. We piled in for the 20-minute ride to the hotel.

"Alright guys, so what's the plan?" Jean asked.

"We're going to get to the hotel, settle in for a few, then go to the Khnum Temple," I said.

Everybody nodded in agreement.

We finally got to our hotel, and Jean checked us in. We went to the suite and put our bags down.

"We have to go now, if I sit down, I'm going to pass out. I was up the whole train ride," I said.

"That's because you slept on the plane," Rosette said.

"I know," I said.

We went to the lobby and asked for a cab to the Temple. They told us that it was only open for another two hours, so we had to hurry. We all piled into the same van as before. What's with these prostitution cars everywhere? We were in the cab for about half an hour until we pulled up. We tipped the guy and stood in the sweltering heat in our hoodies. There were a few guided tours going on. Jean threw a few coins into the water fountain outside. I smiled.

"What's so funny?" he asked.

"Do you even know where that tradition comes from?" I asked.

"I assume I'm about to get a story out of you," he said.

"It turns out that metals such as copper sterilize water. It kills all the bacteria and viruses in the water and makes it safe for consumption. The ancients knew about this, so that's why they did it. You just do it because you're wishing for good luck," I said.

"Interesting Graham, we don't have much time though," Josh said.

I turned and looked at him. Maybe the voice in my head was right. Maybe he was just using us until we gave him what we got. How do we even know if he was officially kicked out of the Masons. All these questions ran through my head until I shook my head back and forth and turned to them all.

"Alright guys. Let's go see what we can figure out," I said.

We walked in past the 6 large columns and began to look around. Saw all of the carvings. Typical Egyptian carvings. The people with the elongated heads. All the hieroglyphs. But nothing out of the ordinary. We spent an hour looking at every carving, some had lizard heads. I laughed at the thought of Reptilians being real, despite what I heard in that channeling of the Pleiadians a while back. Finally, after a while we all met up in the middle of the Temple.

"Did you guys get anything?" Jackson asked.

"Nothing from me," Hannah said.

"Nope," Jean said.

"That's a no from me, too," Larisa said.

Everybody looked at me.

"Ugh God, why do I always have to be the one to figure out the Zodiac stuff? It's so frustrating," I said as I ran my hands through my hair and looked up.

And there I saw it.

There was a huge carving on the ceiling. I carefully looked at every sign and noticed something interesting. There was a Sphinx in between Leo and Virgo.

"Hey guys, look at that," I said and pointed at the location.

Everybody looked up and saw the same thing.

"What does that mean?" Jean asked.

"It's interesting. See in modern astrology, Aries is the first month. It's the Spring, when things come back to life. The Passover, the Resurrection et cetera. However, in astrology the beginning is also in Capricorn, on December 25th, the day the Sun comes back to life. However, in Egypt it was different. The beginning of the Astrological year began in Virgo, the lady with the wheat stalk. That's when all the food was harvested. There's a Sphinx directly between Leo and Virgo here. It's showing that this is the beginning of the year," I said.

"So, what's that mean for us? Is the clue the Sphinx? Is that where we have to go?" Hannah asked.

"Hold on. I'm not entirely sure," I said, as I turned around and started walking around looking some more.

I must have scanned the entire place two more times until we heard an announcement.

"Thirty minutes until closing," the loudspeaker said.

We were really going to have to figure this out. I looked everywhere, I couldn't tell everyone what I was looking for because I didn't exactly know myself, until I finally saw it.

There was a constellation map. Something was bothering me about it until I finally figured it out.

"Hey guys, come here a sec," I turned to everyone.

"First, did everyone hear that announcement?" I asked them. Everybody nodded. I just wanted to make sure I wasn't hearing the voice again.

"OK, so the ancient Egyptians imagined one constellation as a Sphinx. In today's constellation map we call it Centaurus since the Greeks imagined it as a Centaur. If you look right there," I began as I pointed to Libra-Scorpio, "There's a Sphinx in place of the constellation Centaurus," I said.

"So, what you're saying is?" Jackson asked.

"It's the Sphinx. We can get out of here now. We just need to figure out what we need to do with the Sphinx. What was the rest of that riddle?" I asked everyone.

"Locate the difference and seek out Boriska's secret," Larisa said.

"Let's go back to the hotel and figure out exactly who this Boriska is," I said.

We left the Temple and walked towards the cars. There was a cab waiting. I had noticed that when I was pointing to the ceiling that there were some people that were looking at us strangely, but I let it slide. Just thought that it was because we were foreign. Or because we had hoodies on. I didn't know somebody was watching us, and it drastically altered our search for the Library.

The illiterate of the 21st century will not be those who cannot read or write, but those who cannot unlearn the many lies that they have been conditioned to believe, and seek out the hidden knowledge that they have been conditioned to reject—Gavin Nascimento

Chapter Sixteen

Due to some traffic, this time it took half an hour to get back to the hotel. We got to our hotel, and Jean paid the cab driver. We went back in and went up to our room. Once there, we started talking about our next steps.

"So, it is the Sphinx. That's good to know. But what about it? What are we supposed to do? I mean, there's a few entrances to it, one from the back that I'm aware of," Larisa said.

"I'm not really sure, but we need to figure out this Boriska thing, whatever that means. It holds the clue to this all," I said.

"I'll start looking online to see if I find anything," Rosette said.

"I'll help too," Jackson said.

We sat there for a half an hour trying to figure out the secret meaning of the code we were given. So far no luck. It was right then that Josh spoke up and put some pep in our step.

"Guys, we have to get out of here, so please hurry up," he said.

"Why? What's wrong Josh?" I asked.

He pointed at the giant mural painting above the TV.

"Alright so, I don't see anything," I said.

"Count the animals," Josh said.

It took me a few minutes, but I was able to locate them all.

"What's your point?" I asked.

"And Joachim went down right away and summoned his shepherds with these instructions: 'Bring me 10 lambs without spot or blemish, 12 tender calves, 100 goats,' " he said.

"Alright so what's the big deal?" I asked.

"That's from the Infancy Gospel of James 4:5. This hotel is owned by that secret society," he said.

"Really?" Jackson said.

"We've got to go," he said.

We went to the lobby and Josh asked the concierge where they could rent a car. They told him. He and Jean went outside and took a cab to the car rental place. About an hour later they came back with that same creepy looking van. We all brought our bags and piled into the van.

"Alright, so what's next?" Jean asked.

"I think I might have something here guys," Rosette said.

We stopped and turned to her.

"Alright so a few years back there was a kid named Boriska Kipriyanovich who claimed in his past life he was born on Mars," she started.

"I don't believe in past lives, this is stupid," Jean said.

"Whether you believe it or not, this is something that a lot of people do. Anyway, he claimed that when he was a Martian, he flew to ancient Egypt as a pilot. He claimed that the secret to all human life can be found inside the Great Sphinx of Egypt. He even goes so far as to claim that the secret lies behind one of the Sphinx's Ear. That will unlock a secret tunnel that will take you to an unknown chamber," Rosette said.

"Alright. Let's hypothetically say that this Indigo child is right. Is there any reason to believe that there is an opening there?" Larisa asked.

"There is an opening there," Rosette said.

"What?" I asked.

"Look," she said as she showed us this picture she just found.

Sure enough, there was a door letting in through the head of the Sphinx, but it wasn't behind the ear, it was directly under it.

"How are we supposed to get in there exactly?" Jackson asked.

Just then our friend came back to visit.

I hear you're having issues with the door at the Sphinx.

"Yes," I said out loud knowing full well he could hear me. "Did you know about this?" I asked.

I have heard rumors, but your travels so far have lead me to believe they were actually true. You're in

luck. There just so happens to be construction going on at the head of the Sphinx, you should be able to access it pretty easily, if you can figure a way to bypass security. Either that or wait until nighttime.

"I don't know how we're going to be able to get that giant door out of the way," I said.

It's not a door. Well, technically it is a door, but it's made of pure limestone. You will have to find a way to get it open. There is a latch from the inside that has this locked, it's a six-thousand-year-old wooden bolted lock mechanism. You will need to unhinge the latch before you open the door. The door was cut with such precision and has such a perfect center of gravity that once the lock is opened, you should be able to push it open with two hands.

"So how exactly are we supposed to open a lock from the inside of a giant limestone piece?" I asked.

The ancients knew a lot more than you or I did regarding vibrations. It's one of Hermes principles, as I'm sure you know already. Use archaeoacoustics to get the desired outcome.

"Wait! What do you mean by that?" I asked.

He was gone for now.

"Alright guys, what's that thing he said?" I asked.

"It's something called sonic drilling," Jackson began, "The best example would be tuning forks attached to a long copper tube. Has to be a big fork though," he said.

"Explain this to me," I said.

"Alright, so basically they say that tuning forks were invented in 1711, but the Egyptians have had them in hieroglyphs and drawings all the way back then. You put the copper pipe on something, then you smack the tuning fork. The unbelievably quick vibrations of the fork causes the pipe to vibrate the same, in hand turning it into one giant sound drill. It can bore perfect holes. We're going to have to find a giant tuning fork," Jackson said.

"Found it," Rosette said.

We stared at her blankly.

"What? I started looking into this as soon as he started talking. It turns out that this message board talks about how the Cairo University has a room in the basement full of these artifacts that they are trying to keep hidden from the public," Rosette said.

"Why keep something from the public at a University?" I asked.

She shrugged.

"It's more than that though. Based on the size of the limestone and the speed of sound through it, I need to calculate its resonant frequency and make sure we have a tuning fork that can match it," Jackson said.

"How long will that take you to figure out?" I asked.

"Rosette sweetie, can you find the length of an average limestone from the Pyramid?" Jackson asked.

"Um, it says here, hold on, it says here 2.2 meters, so like seven feet about," she said.

Jackson took out his phone and started typing away at it for a few minutes.

"I hope that whatever we have to do at the University, my girlfriend doesn't have to get naked," Jean said.

"Oh get over it sweetie," Larisa said.

"Does your sex life spark joy?" Rosette asked Jean.

"Shut up with your Marie Kondo bullshit Rosette," Jean said.

"Here, I've got it. So the speed of sound through limestone is around 3000 m/s, by my calculation its resonant frequency is about 682 Hz. Which is PERFECT because that's a normal range, we just need to find a big enough tuning fork," Jackson said.

"Anybody have any ideas?" I asked.

"Rosette, can you find out what room these are locked in?" Larisa said as she started playing around with her computer.

"No need to, this person included a map," Rosette said.

"Well that is good news. Getting inside. Ideas people?" I asked.

"What if we brought a bunch of cleaning supplies and went in as janitors?" Jean asked.

"That's actually not a bad idea at all," I said. "Let's go find some garbage bins and supplies," I said.

"Jean looked up a cleaning supply place and we took the 20-minute ride there. We loaded up on large garbage pails and cleaning supplies. He also picked up a few all white janitor outfits. The bad news, the bullet proof sweatshirts won't fit under this. The better news is that I think this will work.

"OK, so for this to work we all need to go inside, it has to look like a team. So here's what we're going to do. Jackson, me and Larisa are going to go inside one of these bad boys and cover it in a garbage bin. When we give the signal, we're going to leave one by one back to the van," I said.

"Fine by me," Larisa said.

"Larisa, do you still have the master thumbprint? Did you bring that with you?" I asked.

"Of course I did. I always have that on me," she said.

"Jackson, are you able to pick out which tuning fork will work?" I asked.

"I'll need 2 minutes, but yes. Also, they should already have the copper tubing attached to it if they really are that ancient," he said.

"You should be able to separate them so it doesn't look like we're obviously stealing something," I said.

"Yeah, they should unscrew," he said.

We all gathered together. We weren't going to have much time to get this done before someone realized something was wrong.

If God created the Mazzaroth for us, the 12 signs of the zodiac; it would only be logical for one to think that he created a completely different type of Mazzaroth for other beings in other star clusters—Unknown

Chapter Seventeen

We pulled up to Cairo University. We all changed into our janitor's clothing in the van. If someone had opened the van at that moment, it would have surely looked like a giant orgy just wrapped up. I opened the door and stepped outside, blinded by the Sun, but a little cooler now that I wasn't wearing the hoodie.

"Alright guys, this is it. Just get some water and mop the floor, look busy until you hear from us," I said as we all put our earpieces back in.

"Roger that team," Jackson said.

We made our way past the very long row of water fountains on the main campus. We went inside and split off into two teams. Josh was waiting in the van in case something came up.

"Alright Rose, what floor do we take this main elevator down to?" I asked.

"It's not the main one, it's the one about 300 yards behind that in the building across," she said as she was mopping the floor.

We walked as she said to the other set of elevators.

"Ok, we're here now, so what now?" I asked.

"Go down to LL2," she said.

We pressed LL2, but it wouldn't let us go down. Someone else came into the elevator and pressed 2. We were going up. They must keep this secure. When this young lady got out of the elevator, she looked at us and smiled. We smiled back.

"Larisa, try the master print," I said.

She pulled out her 3D printed rubberish glove that we had gotten to know so well and pressed her thumbprint on the reading mechanism above the floor numbers. It beeped green and we went down.

We arrived downstairs and got out.

"Alright Rose, where do we go?" I asked.

"Turn left, walk down about 100 yards and it should be a double bolted door," she said.

Sure enough, we got to that location. As we got to that location, there was a double door. Larisa opened the door with her print, and Jackson went in. We shut the door quickly with him still inside as we heard footsteps.

"What are you doing down here?" a man asked as he was coming to me.

"We're the janitors. We're exchange students, we're working here for free tuition," I said as I mopped the floor.

"Alright, but don't stay down here too long. This entire floor locks down in twenty minutes," the man said as he turned around and walked away.

Twenty minutes?

"Jax, we have a problem buddy. You've got about 10 minutes to find this thing, then another 10 to walk back to the elevator. This floor locks down at 4 apparently," I said.

"Almost done my G. I'm just testing a few of these forks out against my phone reader," he said.

We cleaned up that area a bit because we might as well do something while we were waiting. Finally, Jackson came to the door and opened it from the inside. He had a 3-foot tuning fork in one hand and a 4-foot copper barrel in the other.

"You sure this is it?" I asked.

"One hundred percent," he said.

We put the two items in the garbage pail and threw the mop in there and covered it with some towels. Just for good measure, we washed the floor with ammonia to leave a smell in case someone came to check on us. We got back in the elevator with 3 minutes to spare and made our way back to the main level.

"Alright guys, party's over, we need to go," I said.

Josh heard us and drove up to where we were and picked us all up. We took everything with us, so as not to arouse suspicion.

"So what's next?" Jean asked.

"Now, we find a new hotel, and then rest until sundown. Let's drive past the Sphinx though," I said.

We drove through Giza until we came upon the Sphinx.

"Pull over," Larisa said.

Josh pulled over.

"What are you doing?" I asked.

"Hold on a sec," she said as she pulled something out of her pocket.

It was an 84x pocket scope. It can zoom 20 miles and costs less than a gram of weed.

"You have to see this," Larisa said as she gave me the scope.

I looked through the lens and zoomed in. I could see the door under the ear, clear as day.

"How do people not know about this?" I asked.

"I don't know," Larisa said.

"How does this thing even work? The zoom is outrageous on this thing," I said.

"From what I gather, it's through a process known as optical stacking. It combines the power of an optic lens with the digital manipulation of modern camera phones," Jackson said.

I nodded. I looked through it one more time. There was some kind of restoration going on to the Sphinx. There was a giant step system to get up to the top of it, which was a good thing. We didn't need to get Jean's toy from the airplane and have Jackson fly up there and drill.

"We're going to the hotel to wait the rest of the day out," Josh said as he stepped on the gas.

We got to the new hotel and Jean paid in cash. Turns out that if you don't want to use your card, they take cash, double the amount, but still all the same. We got in our room and settled down.

"What these people carried were records of the movement of stars and the constellations," I said.

"What are you talking about?" Rosette asked.

"That was one of Edgar Cayce's readings, 354-4 actually. Talking about the lost information. It's so close I can feel it," I said getting a bit excited. That was immediately shut down by my little friend with me.

I hope you know what you're doing. You can die in there if you're not careful. Nobody would ever find your body.

I shook off the voice and sat down and opened a bottle of water from the refrigerator.

"In those periods when the first change had come in the position of the land, there had been an egress of people from the Atlantean land, and they built a city near the edge of the Sahara. Reading 5748-6," I said.

"I thought this was about the Library of Alexandria?" Hannah asked.

"If he was right, it would be an amalgamation of everything. All their records, all the old lost records, everything," I said.

We talked for a few hours until it got dark. Then we left the hotel and boarded the van. We made our way back to the Sphinx.

There was nobody around it now. We got out of the van and walked over to it and started climbing this ladder system until we got to the top of the head. We took a few minutes to catch our breath. I turned to everyone and pointed out in front of us.

"Hey, did you guys know there was a giant hole in the top of the head of the Sphinx?" I asked.

Everybody shook their head no.

"Well there is," I said.

"We can see that bud," Jackson said.

I turned to Jackson. "Are you ready to go do the work of the Angels?" I asked.

He gave me the thumbs up. He put together the tuning fork and the copper pipe and then made his way down the ladders until he was able to reach the stone that was clearly out of place.

I turned to Hannah and lit a cigarette.

"You know when I get pregnant and it sticks, you're quitting smoking right?" she asked.

I had completely forgotten about that unfortunate event. I must have completely pushed it out of my head. I nodded my head to her and flicked the cigarette over the top of the Sphinx's head. After a few minutes I went to the ladder and looked over to talk to Jackson.

"Hey Jax, how you doing down there?" I asked.

"I've been workin' on the railroad," he began singing.

I pulled my head back up and sat down on the head. Everybody else was talking among themselves. I was just trying to get this voice to go away. I was tempted to pull Rosette aside and let her know exactly what I was going through at that moment, but I figured it would just worry her, and then she'd tell Hannah, and then that would turn into a giant bleep show. If this got any more unmanageable though, I wouldn't have a choice. Finally, after a few minutes, Jackson called up to us.

"OK, it's safe to come down," he said.

One by one, we went down the ladders until we met him at the entrance. He was already standing in it. He helped us climb in, one by one until finally Josh, who was the last one, was in. Jackson, then as predicted, was able to swing this stone mountain very easily, shut it. We turned in.

There was a set of ancient stairs that lead its way down what must have been a hundred feet. When we got to the bottom, we were surprised to see there were torches hanging in the wall. I grabbed one and took out my lighter and lit it up. It went up like a bonfire. We started following this one specific path that it had us on for what seemed like miles. Finally, we came to a door full of hieroglyphs. I put the fire up to it to see what it was.

"Hey guys, you're going to want to check this out," I said to everyone.

Everyone gathered around the torch and looked at it. In the center of it was two hieroglyphs of a Sphinx facing another Sphinx.

"When you think about the ancient history of Egypt, and the Sphinxes that have been found across Egypt, you always find evidence of duality, and that all others can be considered an anomaly. Every time we have to deal with the solar cult, we should discuss one lion and one lioness facing each other, or posing parallel to each other, or sitting in a back to back position. Turns out they're facing each other. That's Egyptologist Bassam El Shammaa," I said.

"What are you saying baby?" Hannah asked.

"Where would you say we are exactly right now?" I asked.

"I'd say about half a mile from the Sphinx, deep underground," Jackson said.

"So we're under the Nazlet As Samaan district," I said.

"Yeah so?" Rosette asked.

"What are you getting at Graham?" Josh asked.

"I think we're currently about to go into the second Sphinx," I said.

Freethinkers are those who are willing to use their minds without prejudice and without fearing to understand things that clash with their own customs, privileges, or beliefs. This state of the mind is not common, but it is essential for right thinking—Leo Tolstoy

Chapter Eighteen

"You can't be serious," Jackson said.

"THE second Sphinx?!" Rosette squealed.

"Makes complete sense. If you enter the other chambers of the first Sphinx, you go underground to many chambers but none that lit this path. Come on guys, the library is just inside," I said.

I pushed the door open, and we looked inside but what we saw bothered us. There was a wealth of gold strewn around like a typical pirate movie. Along the walls were bookshelves made of limestone that stretched as far as the eye could see, but there were no books on them. We came into the middle of the room and saw a table with a scroll on it. I blew the dust off and unrolled it to my horror.

It's one thing for you to seek and not find; it's quite another for you to act this unwisely. Don't you know that I don't really belong to you?

"That's not good," Josh said.

"What do you mean?" I asked.

"That's what Jesus says to Joseph when he's repri-manded in The Infancy Gospel of Thomas. He tells him that he doesn't really belong to him," Josh said. "Also, I don't know what these hieroglyphs mean."

I sat back defeated. Somebody had gotten here before us and cleared everything out. I wasn't sure how I was going to be able to tell this to our computer friend. Then it occurred to me.

"Twelve thousand years ago the Sphinx was built in Egypt. It faced the constellation Leo at the time. A second Sphinx was created and buried, only to be dis-covered now. It HAD to be discovered now, do you want to know why?" I asked.

Everybody nodded.

"Because the opposing sign of Leo is Aquarius, which is the age that we're in now. This Sphinx is literally facing the other Sphinx. That means that this Sphinx we're under right now is actually facing Leo right now," I said.

"What does that mean though?" Rosette asked.

"It means that nothing is an accident. If the books are not here, then they have to have been moved somewhere else. The only thing is that we need to figure out where it went," I said as my mind was distracted by something on the floor. I walked across the room and found what looked like a cell phone on the floor. I picked it up and dusted it off. I tried turning it on. It was already on, it was just on auto wipe.

"Larisa. Is there anything you can do with this? It's deleting itself. This could be our only clue!" I screamed.

She ran over to where I was and took the phone. She tried doing a hard reset on it, but it wouldn't shut down. Finally, after a few minutes, the phone was completely dead.

"I have to get this to my surgical lab asap," Larisa said.

"Is there anything you can do to recover the information?" Hannah asked.

"I can't say for sure. But if this phone is here now that means someone else is either still here or was just here, we need to get the hell out of dodge," she said.

We left the room with the phone and made our way back to the other Sphinx. The torch was slowly starting to die, and we picked up the pace. Finally, we got back and walked up those evil stairs. Hacking away at these steps only made me want to have a cigarette more for some reason.

You're lucky you survived that. Keep this up and you will surely die.

I turned to Rosette and fought off the urge to talk to her about this voice. After about another 25 minutes, we made it back up to the Sphinx. Everybody got on the ladder and started climbing down. Jackson wasn't going to be able to lock it from the inside again, but he did replace the hole that he bore out so it didn't look that the Sphinx had been tampered with. After another 15 minutes, we were back at the Van.

"We have to go back to the hotel," Larisa said, still fiddling with the phone.

"Let's go," Josh said as he stepped on the gas.

Twenty minutes later we were back at the hotel. Everybody was lying in bed except for Larisa. We were exhausted.

"What are you doing there girl?" I asked.

"I'm using a recovery stick to hopefully get the information from the phone," she said.

She went on to explain to me that the recovery stick was something new. It somehow was able to retrieve text messages, programs, emails on the phone. I just hoped that it worked.

"Hey guys, what do you make of those hieroglyphs at the end?" Jackson asked.

"What do you mean?" Hannah asked.

"These," he said as he showed her a screenshot he took of them.

"I'm not really sure, maybe we should ask someone?" Josh said.

We went downstairs to the dining room to get some food because we were starving. We ordered our food, and I showed the waiter the hieroglyphs. He gave me a weird look and walked away. Rosette started laughing.

"What's so funny?" I asked.

"It's ancient hieroglyphs. Do you think the average Egyptian is walking around understanding them? Do you think that all Jews go around speaking and reading Aramaic?" she asked and giggled.

She was right though. It was boneheaded of me to ask. We were going to have to get our answers from a place that we just came from. I whipped out my phone and started looking something up.

"What are you doing now?" Jean asked.

146

"I'm looking up a professor at Cairo University. I need answers to this," I said.

I messed around with my phone for a few and was able to locate a professor that would be able to help us out. We would have to wait until morning though. I shot him a quick email.

We finished dinner and went back upstairs. When we got to the room, there was a note slid under the door. I opened it.

Tread lightly.

I showed everybody. Someone knows we're here. The question is why haven't they come for us yet. We lay down in bed and passed out for the night. Larisa kept working on the phone while we slept.

We awoke in the morning and went downstairs to grab a quick breakfast. Sometime in the middle of the night, Larisa was able to crack it. She showed us the only thing that she found that could be of any relevance.

A map that was written from maps of the Great Library of Alexandria, A home of the Sultans and a low security prison for it. Showing a map of a world already discovered well before it's official discovery. Find the land that's vastly different.

"Before we figure that out, we need to get going to the University," I said as I paid the bill. We took our leftovers and went out to our van. We all piled in and began our short drive over.

We got to the university, and I asked around to Dr. Hassan's office. We were directed over to him. It just so happened we caught him with a few minutes between his classes.

"Hello Dr. Hassan. It's me Graham. I reached out to you last night," I said.

"Very nice to meet you. I only have a few moments. Can you tell me what you need?" he asked.

"I just wanted to show you this and see if you could translate it for us," I said as I showed him.

He put on his reading glasses and took a look. His eyes grew wide and he took his glasses off sharply and stared at me.

"Where did you get this?" he asked.

"It doesn't matter. Can you help us?" I asked.

He looked over to us one by one, looked down at his feet and finally spoke.

"This isn't even supposed to exist," he said.

"What isn't supposed to exist?" Rosette asked.

"This strand," he said. He had a very worried look on his face.

"Professor, please just tell us what it says," Hannah said.

"It's hieroglyphics for something called 'Osirica'," he said.

"What is Osirica?" I asked, as I shot a look over to Josh whose face grew wide and nervous just like the Professor's.

"Your friend seems to know. Why don't you ask him, I have to go," he said as he stood up and left the room with us in it.

"Josh," I began, "what is Osirica?" I asked.

Josh took a deep breath and looked over all of us. "Well," he began.

Every act of conscious learning requires the willing-ness to suffer an injury to one's self-esteem. That is why young children, before they are aware of their own self-importance, learn so easily; and why older persons, especially if vain or important, cannot learn at all
—Thomas Szasz

Chapter Nineteen

"Josh, don't make me keep asking," I said.

Don't ask him again you idiot. It's obviously best you don't know.

"First, Graham, you have to understand a few things about the Masons. We have been around for a very long time. In fact, a poem known as the "Regius Manuscript" dates back to about 1390 and it's the oldest known Masonic text. Osirica predates it by thousands and thousands of years. People think that we're Satanists, elitists, part of the cabal. It's just not true. When a Mason joins, he has to pledge loyalty to something above him, to a higher power, but that is never asked about and discussed. Albert Pike gets a lot of credit for saying that we are all Luciferians or at least at the 33rd degree in the Scottish Rite they are, but that's just his view. Masons do not speak for the views of other Masons. The Catholic

Church has a Code of Canon Law from 1917 barring Masons from joining Catholicism, even though Catholics were never barred from Masonry. In article 28 of its Covenant, Hamas says that Freemasonry is in 'work of the interest of Zionism.' Almost every religion has rules against giving us any credence. However, in the late 70's an Italian Mason chapter nearly bankrupted the Vatican Bank, but that's beside the point. The reason I tell you all this stuff even though I swore to keep it a secret is because Osirica is considered the father of Masonry. These were the people who built all the ancient structures in Egypt that still stand today. They're considered a Black Egyptian masonic order that birthed us. We know they exist because of archeological evidence of an Egyptian village near Deir El Medina. The people that lived there developed their education and minds in let's say a 'unique' way. They were the builders of the Valley of the Kings. They were known as the followers of Isis, the Virgin who bore Horus, the Egyptian Sun God. They worshiped the 'virgin' long before Catholics had an inkling of what they were. The name of the place where they came from was "Set Ma'at" or "the place of truth" it was during Pharoah Amenhotep I, which tells you just how old they are. I can't believe they still exist," he said.

"Why? I don't understand what the problem is," I said.

"You don't get it. This is where everything started. The ancient elite bloodlines, the stories and rumors, if they're real, than the rest must be true. They say Osirica was directly influenced by the gods," he said.

I thought carefully about everything that I had experienced before I threw out the next question.

"How have they been underground this entire time?" I asked.

"How could they not? There're underground bases in Antarctica a mile below the ice where entities live, the government keeps that quiet. Also, come on Graham. You see the hieroglyphs all over the place. The beings with elongated skulls that nobody in the science field wants to talk about. They've recorded it in history. They're throwing it right in your face, and you don't even realize what you're seeing," he said.

We sat there thinking about his rant that he just got finished delivering. Were we way over our heads once again? Probably. Was it too late to stop? The stakes were too high. We had to risk it.

"So what do we do now?" Larisa asked.

"We figure out the next riddle, and I think I know where it is," Josh said as he lead us back to the van for our trip back to the hotel.

After a short ride, we were back in our hotel. We parked and went into our room. God the air conditioning here is divine.

"A map that was written from maps of the Great Library of Alexandria, a home of the sultans and a low security prison for it. Showing a map of a world already discovered well before its official discovery. Find the land that's vastly different," Josh said.

"Anybody have a clue? Jackson asked.

"I think I know," Rosette said shyly.

"Well?" Hannah asked.

"Home of the Sultans is a few centuries old, but it's in Istanbul, Turkey. It's at a place called Topkapi Palace. That's where they used to live," she said.

"Jean, can you make the call?" I asked as I turned to him. He nodded.

"Everything mentions something that came from Alexandria. Did you know that Hypatia of Alexandria was a mathematician, astronomer and philosopher? She taught all these esoteric ancient sciences that keep on coming up with us. She was eventually murdered by a Christian mob. All her works are missing. I can't imagine her works not being in the library, if we ever find it," I said.

"Also, according to Plutarch, Aristarchus postulated heliocentrism well before Julian the Apostate brought it up in his writings. Seleucus of Seleucia who lived a century later confirmed it, but no full records have been found. They must be in the library as well," Josh said.

"God, can you imagine the wisdom that would be in all these works?" Hannah asked.

"Have you guys ever heard of the déjà vu theory?" Jackson asked.

We turned to him.

"It basically says that it's a 'crossover' with a parallel universe. A parallel version of you is doing the same thing in a different universe simultaneously. This is the multiverse hypothesis. There was a stir in the community that said when we started particle accelerating at CERN, we accidentally knocked us into an alternative reality. Doesn't what we're doing sometimes feel surreal or not like we've really experienced everything we've done so far? Like Tesla said, " 'You will live to see man made horrors beyond your comprehension,' " he said.

"For once Jackson, I think I can agree with you on that," I said.

"You're a fan of Tesla?" Josh asked Jackson.

"I wouldn't say so much that I'm a fan of Tesla, rather that I hate Edison," Jackson said.

"Why do you say that?" Josh asked and smirked.

"Where do I begin with Tesla. Well, Edison initially hired him and offered him 50,000 dollars to solve a problem that nobody at his facility could. Tesla did it and Edison remarked that it was "a joke." He then left Edison. Down the road he created something called AC, to compete with Edison's DC. Do you know what Edison did?" Jackson asked Josh.

Josh nodded.

"Exactly. He took an elephant in public and electrocuted it using AC to show the public just how bad it was. That's not all though. He didn't actually invent the lightbulb, he was known to steal or bully people into giving him patents. Do you know why Hollywood is in California?" Jackson asked.

Josh shook his head no.

"Because back at the turn of that century, he held all the electricity, the equipment, everything. The movie studios were getting banged out for their buck by Edison, and he refused to give them a break. They decided before there were airplanes mind you, to go out to California. Go out as far away from Edison and his reach as possible. Yet, in the school systems, all they teach you is about Edison, not Tesla and his free energy machine. In 1890 there was a man named Louis Le Prince, who filmed the first ever motion pictures and disappeared without a trace. Thomas Edison took the credit as the first and sole inventor of cinema and took Le Prince's son to court. A few years later the son died under mysterious circumstances. Screw Edison. Which reminds me, Graham if you still have the President's email, you should tell him to declassify those plans. I know the FBI raided his hotel room when he died and confiscated everything," Jackson said.

"I don't think that's high up on the list of things he'd be dealing with. The vaccine scare is still fresh in his mind," I said.

"Hey Graham," Jackson started.

"Yes Jax?" I asked.

"Remember that book I told you I was reading a while?" he asked.

"Yeah, what about it?" I asked.

"Do you ever get the feeling that the majority of the people you run into day to day can't collapse the wave function?" he asked.

I thought for a minute. "Yeah, the more I learn and get myself into, the more I feel all alone in this," I said.

"But you're not alone baby. You have all of us," Hannah said.

"OK cuties. Playtime is over. The plane will be ready in an hour. Let's go," Jean said.

"What about the van?" Rosette asked.

"I'll email them and tell them it's at the airport. We have to go. I have a strange feeling that we're running out of time," Jean said.

We all got in the van and made our way to the airport. After two trips here, I was so done with Egypt. I didn't know that we were walking right into a trap and that I was going to see my friends die all over again.

If you find from your own experience that something is a fact and that it contradicts what some authority has written down, then you must abandon the authority and base your reasoning on your own findings—Leonardo Da Vinci

Chapter Twenty

We got on the flight to Istanbul. I had never been to Turkey before, the only thing I even know about Turkey is what I saw in Dan Brown's "Inferno." Even that, I don't remember much of it. I used the wifi and Larisa's computer to look up how far the drive from the airport to the Palace was. Turns out it's a 5-minute drive. Literally a 20-minute walk from the airport. Screw it, we're walking I thought. I was about to close the computer when I got an ominous message from our friend.

Where are you off to?

Istanbul. I wrote back in the notepad.

What's in Istanbul?

Apparently, a map that shows something that shouldn't exist.

Tread lightly. They're on to you.

I froze for a moment.

Who?

Osirica. You stirred up an old friend in your travels. Be very careful.

That was the last I heard from him this trip. I thought of his message to tread lightly. Was he the one that left the note under our hotel door?

"Hey guys, our friend sent us a message back," I said.

Everyone turned around.

"We'll let him know when something comes up," Rosette said.

We sat there for a few more moments. We were going to begin our descent shortly.

"Why are you guys so rough on each other?" Josh asked me.

"Because that's the only way we could get through what we've been through," Rosette said.

"You know it girl," Larisa said and blew her a kiss. Rosette giggled.

We began our descent and my ears popped. This happens from time to time when I fly. While I was trying to unclog them, I got a chilling message from within.

This is where you are going to die. You, your friends, you're all going to drown.

I shook off the voice that was now super crystal clear in my head, maybe even clearer than my own thoughts. I was trying not to answer my voice and antagonize it.

There was a war going on in my head and sometimes it was hard to even function on a normal level. When I get back to the United States, I am going to go get some serious help. I don't think anybody has learned or gone through what my friends and I have to this date.

We landed and my ears popped back. That was a good sign. We left our bags on the plane as we weren't planning on being here long. We went through customs and told them we were in town for a friend's party. They let us through. We made the 20-minute walk in about half an hour. God's sun was extremely hot today. Once we got to the Palace, we went in and started looking around.

"Alright so what are we looking for exactly?" Rosette asked.

"You're the one that figured this place out girl. We're looking for something that doesn't fit right," I said.

"Nothing about this entire ordeal fits right," Rosette said.

"You're right about that. Nonetheless we are here, so everybody fan out, and we'll meet back in an hour," Jackson said.

We all split up into pairs, except Josh who was the seventh wheel in our group now. My next mission was going to be to find him a nice girl. At the very least, sign him up on Tinder.

"Baby, I have no idea what we're looking for," Hannah said to me.

"Mrs. Newsdon, I have to ask you," I began as we stopped walking and I turned to her. This was the first time I was alone with her in God knows how long. "Are you, OK?" I asked.

"Yeah why?" she replied.

"No, I mean, are you, OK?" I asked and motioned to her belly.

"It doesn't hurt anymore. I didn't even know I was pregnant, I'm trying not to think about it. To be honest, I'm surprised it hasn't happened before, with you being an expert cocksmith and all," she said smiling at me.

"Well I mean, is this something that you want eventually?" I asked.

She looked at me and bit her bottom lip and smiled at me. The single handed most sexy thing a girl can do is bite her bottom lip and look at you. Truth is, I felt a sigh of relief knowing that one day she would want to have a family with me. I have a lot of growing up to do and we keep getting in these situations where we almost die but, besides that, I think that we can eventually settle down.

"OK, just checking sweetie. That means a lot to me," I said.

"No problem sweetie. I'm just glad Larisa gave us those hoodies when she did," Hannah said.

"Me too," I said.

We turned around and kept looking around. I tried to use my extended knowledge of the ancients and the texts to see if something was off, but there was nothing that I could see. After an hour and frustrated, I made my way back to my friends.

"Did you guys see anything?" I asked.

"Negative," Jackson said.

"Nope, but then again it all looks strange to me," Josh said.

"Ugh. Let's split up again and comb through this entire place. I'm going to ask that tour guide over there if she speaks English of course about a map that doesn't exist," I said as I grabbed Hannah and walked away from everybody.

"Excuse me miss, do you speak English?" I asked.

"I do," she said.

"Are there any maps here that shouldn't be here?" I asked.

"No sir. All maps that are here belong here," she said.

"I see. No, I think you're misunderstanding me. I mean, are there any maps that are on display here that show an ancient world or a world that shouldn't exist?" I asked.

She shook her head no.

"Great. Thank you for your time," I said as I turned around.

"Wait," she started as I turned back around "the Curator, Dr. Thabeet should be here shortly. Maybe he would have a better understanding than I do," she said.

"Thank you, I will keep my eye out for him," I said.

We made our way back to the group. It had only been about 20 minutes, but everybody was waiting for us listening to Jackson.

"See the thing is that NASA says that it is possible that we are living in God's computer. It's the holographic theory. The problem is that one day, maybe a few hundred years from now, maybe less, something greater than computers will be created. It will be the hot new thing. Like the printing press revolutionized reading, like airplanes revolutionized travel. It will transcend our universe. Then we'll have to adjust the meaning of it all and our theories on God tailored to that new creation," Jackson said.

"What are you guys talking about?" I asked as I pulled up.

"Don't worry about it. What did the lady say?" Jackson asked.

"She said to wait for the curator to come," I said.

We waited around for a few hours. Yes, hours. Finally, the place was about to close for the night when a man in a tweed suit with a hat and a pipe came up to us. And I thought Sherlock Holmes was dead.

"Hello all. We're closing soon. Is there something I can help you out with?" he asked.

"We're here for a map that's not supposed to exist," Jean said.

"Supposedly it shows a land that shouldn't be there," Larisa said.

"Do you have something here that fits that description?" Rosette asked.

The man took a puff on his pipe, then frowned at it, turned it upside down and smacked the bottom of the pipe. A piece of tobacco fell out. Maybe it was hashish. Not sure. He took a wad in a plastic bag out of his pocket and packed it again. He lit it and took a puff of it. He blew it out and filled the area with sweet smelling smoke. It was definitely hashish.

"We might have something here like that, but it's not open to the public usually. May I ask who you are?" Dr. Thabeet asked.

"We are fellows at an American University doing a group project," I said.

Dr. Thabeet scanned us each individually with his eyes up and down. "You're a long way from home kids," he said.

"Yes we are. Please Doctor, we don't have a lot of time, we have a flight to catch," Hannah said.

The Doctor took another puff of his pipe, staggered back a step, then caught his balance. Hashish was some strong stuff from what I've heard. People are into so many strange things. I remember reading about how in the early 19th century people had something called snuff, which was basically a white powder like cocaine that you snort, but its purpose was to make you sneeze. Something about sneezing back then, like an addictive aphrodisiac. Hash was never my thing though, although I have been to a few hookah bars in my day. I looked at the Doctor and he was staring at me puffing furiously on his pipe.

"Alright, follow me," he said.

We walked to the back of the room and in through a door, took a long hallway back and entered a room. This room was climate controlled. I didn't think they had that kind of technology here. I know they're a modern world, but I had the desert third world mentality for some reason. Dr. Thabeet went into one of the locked cabinets and pulled out a giant scroll made out of what looked like animal skins.

"You kids are familiar with the map of the world, right?" he asked.

I nodded.

"Well this was a map that was created in the year 1513 by Piri Reis. He supposedly created it using a bunch of maps from the ancient times. One of them was from Christopher Columbus," he began.

All at once it clicked. I knew exactly where this was going. "The interesting thing about this map is that it shows the coasts of most of the World as mapped out. But how did they know this back then without satellite imaging? Also, here is the most interesting part," he continued as he took another puff of his pipe, "You see this at the bottom of the map?" he asked.

"What is it?" Jean asked.

"It's Antarctica," I said.

Dr. Thabeet looked over at me and smiled. "You are correct. Now here's the interesting part. This map was created to reflect how the ancients saw the world. This map, the Piri Reis map was created in the 1500's. Antarctica was not officially discovered until the 1800's. Why is Antarctica not covered with ice? Was Antarctica a living breathing body of land at some point in our not too distant past?" he asked.

Showing a map of a world already discovered well before it's official discovery. Find the land that's vastly different. I thought to myself. This has to be it. The library is hidden somewhere in Antarctica, I thought.

"I have a question," I began, "In Antarctica are there any pyramids?" I asked.

Dr. Thabeet looked over at me and puffed on his pipe, "I'm not really an expert on Antarctica. But from what I've learned, there might be or there might not be. Why do you ask?" he asked.

"No reason at all, thank you for your time Dr. Thabeet. May I take a picture of this map?" I asked.

"Absolutely, but keep your flash off. The light could disturb this ancient map," he said.

I snapped a picture with my phone. I motioned to everyone that it was time to go. We all collected and went back out into the main room and started to walk outside.

"What now?" Jean asked.

"We need to figure out where in Antarctica it's hidden. We can't do that here. Let's go back to the plane and regroup," I said.

"Agreed," Larisa said.

We started to walk outside where we were met by two men with guns. We turned around and looked back inside and saw Dr. Thabeet nodding to them, puffing on his pipe. He turned around and went back in.

"We need to have a little talk," one of them said.

We weren't wearing our bullet proof hoodies anymore, and I wasn't going to risk any of my friends lives again, so we followed them and split up into two cars. I had no idea what was coming.

We are drowning in information, while starving for wisdom—Anonymous

Chapter Twenty-One

I woke up tied to a chair in a dimly lit room. At first confusion hit me like a ton of bricks, then I realized that they must have knocked us out. I didn't feel like anybody hit me, so that's a good thing. Anytime you can avoid getting your ass kicked is a beautiful thing. I was a little drowsy though. I looked around and examined my surroundings. Josh was tied up in a chair to the left of me, nobody else was here. I had a feeling in my gut of sheer panic when I realized my wife wasn't around. We were deliberately placed in front of a giant window facing another room, but that room was completely dark. I shook my head a few times to shake off the wooziness, but it seemed to make it a little bit worse. Josh was still knocked out cold. It was just me and my thoughts. Great, I thought.

Look what you got yourself into dumbass. You're so stupid. Whatever happens to you, I bet you deserve every second of it.

I shook off the voice, very careful not to answer it. After a few seconds it seemed to go away. Why couldn't this voice tell me nice and sweet things? I think I could get used to a voice in my head that said wonderful things all the time. A thought entered my head that I might actually be schizophrenic. I don't know why it didn't come to me until now, but it's there. I seem to function neurotypically in other ways, except for the whole get kidnapped thing every once in a while. I was going to have to pull Rosette aside when I had a chance to talk to her about this. Well, first I was going to have to find her then I would talk to her. Where the hell are we anyway?

No sooner had I asked that question to myself when I heard the door open behind me and a person walked in. I heard his boots clump on the marble floor as the footsteps grew closer. The person then walked around the corner and my jaw dropped.

"Hello Graham. So nice to see you again," Dr. Hassan said.

He looked me over and shined a light in my eye to check my dilation. After he was satisfied with the results, he looked over at Josh and frowned. He pulled a smelling salt ampoule from his pocket and snapped it under his nose. Josh woke up in an instant.

"Hello Josh. Tell me, how did you get involved with Graham and his traveling circus?" Dr. Hassan asked.

"I'm sorry Dr. Hassan?" Josh asked.

Dr. Hassan tossed his smelling salts into the garbage can next to Josh. "You can call me Sir Ciao," he said and smiled.

Josh shot me a blank stare. I never told them about the Sir Ciao part. I don't really understand it. Wasn't sir the man from before?

Then it hit me at once. Sir Ciao is an anagram for Osirica. The one that's been in communication with us, who keeps the balance, warned me that they have been on to us for a long, long time. Dr. Hassan saw my face and must have realized that I had figured it out.

"You're a lot brighter than you look Mr. Newsdon. I'll admit I didn't know what to make of you when I saw you walk through my door. You've stirred up a lot of controversy with your books about the Pyramids and such. But to see you there with our name in hieroglyphs, I had to excuse myself from the room. It was too much to bear," Dr. Hassan said.

"What do you want from us?" Josh asked.

Dr. Hassan turned sharply to Josh.

"You are another story. You abandoned everything that you had going for you. 'To all which I do most solemnly and sincerely promise and swear without the least hesitation, mental reservation, or self evasion of mind in me whatever; binding myself under no less penalty than to have my left breast torn open and my heart and vitals taken from thence and thrown over my left shoulder and carried into the Valley of Jehosaphat, there to become a prey to the wild beast of the field, and vulture of the air, if ever I should prove willfully guilty of violating any part of this my solemn oath or obligation of a Fellow Craft Mason; so help me God, and keep me steadfast in the due performance of the same.' Well? Does any of that ring a bell to you? Do you remember saying those words, swearing an oath to the Masons that you would keep all secrets to yourself until the day you die. One that you have brutally violated time and time again. Tell me, should I cut your heart out and drain your blood as you promised?" Dr. Hassan asked.

Josh looked at him blankly, and then put his head down in shame.

"The Osiricans no longer control every aspect of Masonry. Although it owes homage to its creation to us, they are functioning independently now. We don't meddle. But every once in a while someone makes a big stir about it and he has to be dealt with," Dr. Hassan said.

Just then we heard a voice from a loudspeaker creak and a voice came in. An older woman's voice, incredibly distinct.

"Will the matter be completely destroyed or not?" the voice said.

Dr. Hassan dropped what he was doing and looked up at the speaker, trembling.

"That's the opening line of the Gospel of Mary," Josh turned and whispered to me.

"What penance do I owe you for your presence your grace," Dr. Hassan said.

Josh and I looked at each other confused.

"Nothing ever goes away until it teaches us what we need to know," the voice said.

"Understood," Dr. Hassan said.

"Make sure you get it back and make your way over immediately to the Saline Beach across from the broken shelf," the voice said.

"I'm midsemester at work Lady Pindar," Dr. Hassan said.

Josh shot me a look like we were about to die.

"The Pindar is the person at the top of the top of the top as far as running the show for everything," he whispered to me.

"You mean . . ." I asked.

He nodded.

"Don't worry about work. You're on a sabbatical now. I will handle the details. Just make sure it's done. I don't have anyone I can spare as of now besides your team," the voice said.

"You have my word. Thank you, your grace," Dr. Hassan said as he turned back to us. The voice disappeared.

"Why are we here?" I asked.

"You're here because you naughty ones have something that we need. How was Egypt by the way?" he asked.

Josh and I looked at each other and then back at him.

"You don't think we know? We know that you found the second Sphinx. More importantly you found something in there that doesn't belong to you. We need it back now. Now, which one of you is going to get it for us?" he asked.

Again, Josh and I looked at each other not knowing what he was talking about.

"It seems you have come in possession of some very dangerous information about our Lady Pindar. Some information that could bring down the entire operation of how every society works in the world," he said as he turned on the lights in the room we were facing. It was dimly lit, but there, clear as day, we saw all of them tied to chairs, still knocked out.

I struggled to break my restraints, but these twist ties were too strong.

"Which one of you is going to give it back to us. We don't want to hurt you, but believe me, we will," Dr.

174

Hassan said. With that he flipped a switch and water started pouring into the room from the ceiling. "You have about 5 minutes before that room completely fills up with water and your friends drown. If I were you, I would start talking," he said smiling.

I looked across the divider and saw the water rising rapidly.

"We have no idea what you're talking about," I said.

"You don't have a lot of time boys, if I were you, I would quit messing around," Dr. Hassan said.

I looked back at the room. It was about a quarter full of water. They were still unconscious. This wasn't good at all.

"What are you looking for exactly?" Josh asked.

Dr. Hassan looked at both of us then started to laugh to himself. "You mean, you don't actually know that you have it?" he asked, as he continued to laugh.

I looked back at the room and it was about 40% full at this point. The water was up to their knees. Why weren't they waking up.

"How do I even know they are alive at this point?" I asked pointing to them.

Dr. Hassan frowned. "We have a trust here Graham. You must believe it. What did you find in the second Sphinx?" he asked.

I looked over to them, it was up to their belly buttons at this point. I closed my eyes and took a deep breath.

Good job you fucking idiot. You got them all killed. Hope you can live with yourself.

I opened my eyes, that wasn't helping. I tried to think back to if we took anything when it suddenly hit me. The cell phone. I turned to Dr. Hassan and smiled. This caught him completely off guard.

"I remember now," I said smiling.

Dr. Hassan must have thought I was crazy smiling like the Joker at him when my friends were about to drown. But I knew I had the upper hand, and if this had the information on it that I thought it did, we already backed it up.

"I'll get you your phone back, but first turn off the water," I said.

Dr. Hassan scratched his beard and looked over to me. "You get one chance kid. You mess this up, your friends die," he said.

I nodded.

Dr. Hassan turned off the water just as it was reaching their shoulder blades. He then cut my restraints off my feet but kept my hand ones on. I rubbed my wrists as they were ungodly sore. I looked over to Josh.

"I'll be back in an hour," I said.

I turned back to Dr. Hassan.

"Where is it?" he asked.

"It's on Jean's plane at the airport. Where the hell are we exactly?" I asked.

"Follow me," Dr. Hassan said.

I turned back to Josh to let him know everything was going to be OK.

I followed Dr. Hassan to the car in the lot. Alfa Romeo. Not too expensive for a Professor who's in a secret society.

We drove for half an hour until we got to the airport. I walked up to the plane and waved at the pilot who was inside. He lowered the door.

"Alright kid, no funny games. In and out," Dr. Hassan said as he cut my restraints. Finally, blood circulation again in my life.

I slowly climbed up the plane steps until I got in the cockpit. I had about 90 seconds to figure something out. I reached into the bag and got the phone, made sure it still turned on, then turned it off. Then it clicked. I opened Larisa's computer and typed a quick note to the man who was monitoring us. I then shut the computer and walked back down the steps and back to Dr. Hassan. He took the phone from me and turned it on. He smiled when he saw what it was.

"You know, when we were there and left, I figured the phone would die and nobody would ever be able to get to it. Until you and your friends showed up," Dr. Hassan said as he put his seatbelt on and shifted into first gear.

We got back to the location in 45 minutes. There was traffic this time around. I finally got a look at where we were. It was an incredibly unsightly building on the outside. Looked like it belonged in Slumdog Millionaire. I followed him inside and back to Josh.

"I was beginning to get worried you wouldn't be coming back," Josh said.

"Nonsense. Unfortunately, now I have some bad news. It seems like I've gotten a message from the Pindar that we cannot let you go," Dr. Hassan said.

"What?" I asked.

"I'm sorry, this is just the breaks of the business. What the Pindar says, goes. That goes for every single person on this planet. The Royal Family, the President of the United States, everybody. I'm sorry," Dr. Hassan said as he left the room and shut the door.

I turned back and looked at my friends and something was definitely off, they were moving around but they were still sleeping. Am I hallucinating this? After a minute or two more, Dr. Hassan came back in the room, this time with a gun.

"I'm sorry I have to do this to you people," he said.

"So they're going to die for nothing?" I asked as I pointed to my friends through the window.

"Oh that, it's not exactly what you think," Dr. Hassan said as he flipped a panel in the wall and punched in a few codes. All at once my friends fuzzied out and disappeared from their chairs. "That was just the holographic projection of them that we looped while you were knocked out. See, our rules are that we cannot murder anyone directly, but left for dead is another thing," Dr. Hassan said as he aimed the gun at my stomach.

All of a sudden we heard a whack of a metal bat against a skull, and Dr. Hassan crumpled to the floor. Then a tall muscular boy, who I swear could have been Jackson's stunt double, gave him one more on his head for good measure. Blood started pooling from his head as his body twitched. The man dropped the bat on the floor.

"I'm sorry it took so long for me to get here. There was traffic," the man said.

"Who are you now?" I asked.

"My name doesn't matter. What matters is that you reached out to us, and we're here to help. We're only allowed to interfere with the order of things once and only because we're completely confident you're all on the right track. Unfortunately, this uses up your genie wish," the man said.

Then the man rolled Dr. Hassan's body over and started patting him down. He pulled out a gold key and started looking around the room. He walked to the back corner and put the key in it. He opened what became a door where my wife and my friends were. In a concrete box and sweating to death and looking like they just got busted crossing the border. Even though it was sunset, the sun was too bright for them.

"How did you know?" I asked.

"You sent the watcher a message on the computer. Until now you've declined to ask for help. We keep the balance. We don't tilt it one way or another. That is not our job," he said. He walked back over to Dr. Hassan and pulled out the phone. Unfortunately, it had smashed when he hit the floor. The man looked disappointed. He turned to us.

"Did this man say anything to you, or a person he was talking to?" he asked.

"No. Oh wait, something about 'going to the Saline Beach across from the broken shelf,'" I said.

The man looked at us and at Dr. Hassan again. "This body is going to smell like something else in this heat in no time. I suggest we get out of here. Unfortunately, it looks like you are on your own again," he said.

He got into his car and left. I looked around. I didn't have any clue where we were. We started walking in a direction of the nearest town. Once we got there after a brutal 40-minute walk, we flagged down a few cabs and took them directly to the airport. I had enough of Istanbul. We just needed to figure out where we were going next, and it was to the last place any of us would have ever expected.

Every act of conscious learning requires the willingness to suffer an injury to one's self-esteem. That is why young children, before they are aware of their own self-importance, learn so easily; and why older persons, especially if vain or important, cannot learn at all—Thomas Szasz

Chapter Twenty-Two

"Guys, we ready to tell the pilots where we're going in the next half an hour, or they're going to hole up in Istanbul for the night. After our day here, I'm sure none of you want this," Jean said from his normal seat in the plane.

"I know, but the only thing we have to go on is 'Saline Beach across from the broken shelf', I can only assume it's a pyramid or a mountain based on Dr. Hassan's information," I said.

"I'll look up all I can find on Antarctica right now," Rosette said as she started typing away on Larisa's computer.

"Nah Rose, I need you for a minute," I said as I cocked my head and indicated that I needed her in the back of the plane.

She looked at me quizzically and then handed the computer off to Larisa and walked back to me.

"What's up Newsdon. Everything ok?" she asked.

"Actually, it's not. Between my mom passing, the stresses we've been under. Um, I don't know how to say this, but after the Minnesota quiet room, something snapped in my head and I've been uh, hearing voices in my head," I said.

Rosette's look was incredulous. "What kind of voices?" she asked.

"Bad ones," I said.

"What are they telling you right now?" she asked.

Strangle her. Just pop her little neck off like a bottle rocket.

"It's telling me to kill myself," I said.

Rosette looked at me. "I'm going to need a drink, be right back," she said as she walked to the front of the plane and took the bottle of wine out of Hannah's hands and brought it back to me.

"You mean to tell me that you've had voices in your head since Minnesota?" she asked.

I nodded.

"Graham, this is not good. We should go straight back to Boston and get you taken care of. I did tell you when all this began that I wanted you to take the Minnesota test," she said.

I know she was concerned because she called me Graham. She never does that.

"I think I've already been tested in Minnesota plenty, thank you," I said.

"No Graham. For a long time I've wondered about you. Schizophrenia usually manifests in the early twenties. If this is the case, we can't keep going," she said.

"We have to go, we're too close. I'm just going to have to deal with it. Look, I could have kept this to myself until we got back, but I wanted you to know because I really respect your opinion and psych views. We're going to finish this and then I'll get help," I said.

She took a giant gulp out of the bottle and looked me over.

"If that's what you want. I haven't seen you act on your voices, though now that I'm thinking about it, I can tell that something was up. You'd randomly make a sour face or shake your head or put your hands up on your head and rub it. Aw Graham, I'm so sorry I didn't notice this earlier," Rosette said beginning to get teary eyed.

"Don't you dare cry now Rose, you couldn't have known. The truth is, with everything we've been through, I should have been in therapy or medicated a long time ago. We all should," I said.

"Hey guys, I think I have something," Larisa said.

We looked at each other and nodded and walked back to everyone.

184

"Everything ok you two?" Hannah asked as she motioned for Rosette to hand her the bottle back, which she did.

I nodded.

You're going to die with this as your secret.

I shot a look to Rosette to let her know it was back, and she nodded.

"Let's not worry about us for right now. What do you have Riss?" Rosette said.

"I've been looking at Antarctica and everything that they've found on it. There're some serious conspiracy theories that there are aliens that live deep below the surface in American military bases. That aside, there are a few mountains there throughout. But here's the interesting part. The broken shelf part. There's something called the Larsen C ice shelf that broke off the left tip of Antarctica. It's a trillion tons. A TRILLION! Across from it on the other side are a few mountains. Thing is I don't know if this is the place. There are plenty of other mountains and locations in Antarctica, but nothing with a shelf. What do you think that bitch meant by Saline Beach? There's clearly no beaches in this frozen wasteland," she said.

"Who has a base there?" I asked, rubbing my head as the voices were starting to get more frequent.

"It looks like Chile. They have something there called Yelcho Station. It's where the scientists are," Larisa said.

"Give me a pen," I said.

Jackson handed me a pen and a piece of paper. I started rubbing my temples again and took a deep breath. I could see Rosette out of the corner of my eyes getting seriously worried.

"Guys, getting to Antarctica is going to be a pain. There's something called the Antarctic Treaty System that regulates international relations with Antarctica. Countries can't set up military bases there, or claim it as their own. Travel there is completely regulated and forbidden for civilians. No fly zone, no exploration. You can't dock on land," Larisa said.

"That's going to be a problem for us, first because even if we could go there, it's not like there's a runway where I can store the plane. Second, I have to log all flights with the FAA, at least my pilots do. Based on what you said, there's no way we'll be able to fly to Antarctica," Jean slumped.

"We've got bigger problems. We need to figure out where in Antarctica we're going. These kind of things have never stopped us before," Jackson said.

"It is where Larisa said it was," I said after a minute. I was getting a splitting headache at this point. I considered grabbing the bottle of wine from Hannah and pounding the rest of it. That's always made me feel better, well at least until the morning when I would get double anxiety and take a while to get myself together. Rinse and repeat.

"How do you know Graham?" Josh asked.

"Because everything has always been an anagram since this began, so I just needed some information about this. Saline Beach is an anagram for Chilean Base. It seems that no matter how evil it gets, it's still always about anagrams, Bible references, astrology, astronomy, whatever, and they always have to live within their own rules. That's why we've been able to get as far as we have and that's why we'll figure this out," I said.

"Got something else. How exciting!" Larisa said as she laughed.

"What my love?" Jean asked.

"It looks like timing couldn't be better for us. Apparently the first ever 'Flat Earth Society' cruise to Antarctica to find the edge of the world is about to take off from Argentina and the Strait of Magellan in 2 days," Larisa said.

"That's great. Wait, why is it great?" Jackson asked.

"Because it just so happens that that location is directly above the Yelcho Station. If we can only convince them to let us tag along and drop us off and pick us back up, we should be fine," Larisa said.

"That's a great idea, except they're not going to do that. They're not going to cater to 7 crazy people that want to be dumped in Antarctica," Jackson said.

"Money talks," Jean said.

"What's your plan Jean?" Rosette aside.

"Offer them a ton of money to do this," Jean said.

"Do we really want to get involved with the Flat Earth Society right now?" I asked.

"You got any better ideas?" Hannah asked.

"Well no, it's just that, that's the one thing that Blur refuses to talk about," I said.

Everybody looked at me.

"Fine. We'll go to Argentina. But we're going to need to pick up some serious winter clothes, a giant tent and food for the trip," I said.

"Well ahead of you bud. I'm already looking into having Amazon deliver everything to the airport," Larisa said.

"Alright, so it's settled then right?" I asked.

Everybody nodded.

I got up and walked to the back of the plane and cracked myself a beer. Rosette seeing me stood up and walked back to me. She took the beer out of my hands and placed a pill in my palm.

"What's that?" I asked.

"My favorite flight treats," she said.

It was a Xanax.

"I know this isn't going to help with the voices, but it will relax you. You should have seen yourself before, Newsdon. You were basically trembling before. This should take the edge off," she said.

I looked at the pill and popped it. I washed it down with the beer I grabbed back from Rosette's hands. I sat down on the chair and pounded the rest of the beer. I let out a loud belch. Everybody looked at me.

"Guys, I'm fine," I said.

Truth was I wasn't fine at all. I haven't even had time to mourn my mom, I was just thrust directly back into the mix of things. It was also killing me that I hadn't told my wife what was going on with me, but I couldn't risk that right now. We knew that the location of the Library of Alexandria was in a mountain near the Yelcho Station on the tip of Antarctica. We didn't know if people were already there. That Pindar lady did mention that she didn't have a team to go there and God knows if she tried to reach out to Dr. Hassan again. This was almost over, and as soon as I was done, I was going to get help back in Boston.

Hello team, just wondering where you're at right now.

"He's back," Larisa said.

I walked over to the computer and sent him a message.

We thank you for the help you've provided so far and for saving our lives. We know that you can't help us any further. We are just grateful that you did before. We have located the Library of Alexandria, it is in a remote location in Antarctica. We have a plan to get there, not sure if we'll have service or signal while we're there. Will keep you posted when we can. I'll send you the coordinates shortly.

After a few minutes we got a reply.

Always glad to help. We are thrilled that you found the location. We will allow you a week's time there to collect as much information as you can about whatever you want before we relocate it. I look forward to the location. Thank you for all your help, you have no idea what a service you have done to the World.

I walked back to my chair and sat down. The Xanax was starting to affect me a little bit for some reason. I always thought I was immune to Xanax but guess not. The last thing I heard before I fell asleep was Jean telling the pilots where we were going. I passed out, like I hadn't done in forever. Only in my dreams can the voices not get to me.

Go easy on yourself. You are clearing thousands of years of outdated conditioning—Paulina Serafina

Chapter Twenty-Three

I woke up midflight to South America. It seems that it's only when I wake up, for that first few moments, that I am truly at peace. I guess that's what I chase when I drink or when I force myself to sleep when something bad happens. It seems like it's the only thing that works. Also, the voices do not come to me for a few minutes in the morning. Other than that, it's constant. I have only given you a glimpse into what they say to me, otherwise I wouldn't be able to tell the story. I looked over and everybody was asleep. We were somewhere above the Atlantic Ocean at this point. I stood up and cracked my back, neck and knuckles. I walked up to the pilots and asked them how much time we had left. They told me another 5-6 hours. I came back to my chair and sat down and opened a book. I can't remember the last time I actually read a book. After NP died, I became completely obsessed with Religion, Astronomy, Astrology. Rosette would say that psychologically, it was my way of keeping him alive but, the truth of the matter is that, had I not, we wouldn't be where we were and that fact was not lost on me. To be honest, I'm surprised that I've actually lasted this long. There have been so many close calls in the last few years, so many attempts at our lives that I was at the point where I was going to swear off this whole thing. After the Library of Alexandria, I was going to stop giving lectures and even going on these wild goose chases. The truth of the matter is the people who believe my stories will believe me. The ones who cling on to their religion and what have you, will continue to do that. No matter how much I scream at the top of my lungs, nobody is going to change their mind unless they want to. I've made enough of a splash and now with my books being turned into a movie series, it will only further divide people. So is human nature. No matter who or what comes to me, this was it. I'm not a superhero, in fact I am a broken person, with a serious mental health issue. I'm just surprised that I've been able to function this far. Do you have any idea how exhausting it is to constantly be fighting with a voice in your head? It drains the life out of you. By 10 a.m. I'm completely exhausted. I just have to keep pushing through. Truthfully, unless you've experienced it, you can't fully understand it. Rosette with her psych degree and eventually becoming a psychiatrist, though she can understand symptoms, can't walk a mile in my shoes. Honestly, I'm a little worried about whether Hannah is going to be able to handle such a difficult thing, or if she will retreat into herself. If we all get out of this alive, after I get fixed, we're going on a long vacation. Screw it, I might have Jean just buy an Island and live there with all of them for the rest of our lives. It's not like he can't do it. I am glad that Rosette has finally welcomed him back to us. It took us a long time to get back to where we were before NP's death. But it's not like he hasn't paid his way back in literally and figuratively. He saved my life with Marshall in Jerusalem. To be honest, I'd rather have a mental problem and 6 amazing people in my life, than to not have it and have nobody in my life. This is my family that we're talking about at this point, and I was going to protect them at all costs.

"What are you doing baby?" Hannah yawned and asked me.

"Just writing some notes for the next book," I said.

"But the story is not over yet," she said.

"It's just, our lives are so crazy. I mean, who would believe these stories that we've been through the last few years unless someone wrote them down. I just never thought it would turn into this," I said.

"Well, what did you expect to happen?" Hannah asked.

"Honestly, I thought that I was going to change the world," I said.

"Honey, we are changing the world, everything from taking down the President, to the Pyramid lights, to the communication device, to saving everyone from that evil poison in the vaccine, to getting the Library of Alexandria back. How exactly have you not affected the world?" she asked.

I hadn't thought of it like that. I was so pre-occupied with worrying about whether people realize that we are controlled by the celestial bodies in the sky that I didn't stop to think just how much we accomplished. Any one of those things she mentioned would have been a lifetime achievement for anybody. We had a bunch of them. It was the norm for us.

"What are you two talking about?" Rosette asked as she woke up.

"Nothing much, just random stuff," she said.

"OK, wake me up when we get to South America," she said as she went back to sleep.

I turned to Hannah, and we talked for another two hours. The voices were starting to make me tired again, so I told her goodnight and forced myself back to sleep. Chasing that 5 minutes of morning glory is exhausting.

We were awakened as the plane descended and my ears popped. I popped a piece of gum in my mouth and chewed on it and my ears popped back. It was the only trick I knew.

"Alright so I'm told that they're holding our stuff at the Rio Grande Airport where we're scheduled to land in 20 minutes," Larisa said as she fastened her seatbelt.

One by one, everybody started waking up and realizing we were in our descent. I turned to Rosette and nodded to her and motioned popping a pill. She got the message.

We had a bumpy landing, but other than that we were fine. We got off the plane and walked to customs. We cleared quickly and grabbed our stuff that we had sent. Jackson had a giant bag with our tent in it, Josh carried the dry food that we ordered. The girls took the rest of the stuff.

We hailed a cab to where the yacht was docked. Took about 35 minutes. Once we got there, we walked up to the man taking names and letting people on the boat.

"OK everybody, please give me your name and who referred you to our adventure," the man said.

How were we going to get on?

We got to the front of the line after a 30-minute wait. Finally, Jean spoke to them.

"Guys, we have a request that we really need your help with," Jean began.

"What is that?" the man asked.

"If you go straight South from here, you will hit the tip of Antarctica. We desperately need to get there. Are you able to give us a lift and drop us off and pick us up?" Jean asked.

"Are you punking me right now?" the man asked.

Jean shook his head no.

The man looked around and then burst out laughing. Not a good sign.

"You've got to be kidding me. We absolutely can't do that. Who are you anyway?" the man asked.

I pushed my way to the front.

"Listen sir, I know this is unconventional, but you are our one and only hope to reach Antarctica. There's something that we need to do there. Please, we'll do anything," I said.

"Look, I don't know who you guys are, but this is a serious expedition right now we're about to embark on. We're not a taxi service. I'm going to have to ask you to leave," the man said.

Just as the man was waving security to get rid of us a man came up to us.

"Are you Graham Newsdon?" this young person asked.

"I am," I said.

"Oh man, wow. I didn't know you were a truther," the kid said.

I thought about arguing it, but right now I was trying to get on board.

"You know these people?" the man asked.

"Of course. He's a legend in Ft. Lauderdale. I've seen all your lectures online dude. I'm Max," he said.

"Graham," I said as I shook his hand.

"The problem is they're not with us Max they want to be dropped off in Antarctica," the man said.

Max looked at us and then smiled. "No freaking way. You're on the hunt for something are you? Going to be in your next book? I can't wait to read it.

"Get us on this boat and get them to drop us off and I'll mention you in it," I said.

The kid's eyes lit up. "Oh man, you came to the right place. My dad is the Captain of this ship. Just tell me what you want, and we'll make it happen. Follow me," he said as he cocked his head nudging us to climb on board.

We walked past the man with the clipboard. Rosette stuck her tongue out at him. Typical Rose.

"We walked for what seemed like hours. This was a fun cruise. It wasn't just a Deadliest Catch. We finally came up to a room with your stereotypical Titanic captain sitting in his chair. Maybe I shouldn't have made that comparison right now actually.

"So you're the one that my son watches all day on AquaStream. I'm Andreas," he said.

"Hi Andreas. Your son tells me that you guys can help us," I said.

"What did he say?" he asked.

"We need to go to the Yelcho Base Mountain across from the Larsen C ice shelf," I said.

Andreas looked us all over.

"I'm not going to ask what you're doing there, but is it illegal?" he asked.

"The only thing we're not supposed to do is literally be there. But aside from that it's fine," Josh said.

"I can get you there. It'll take 2 days. The only thing is that we can't do it for free, if you know what I mean," Andreas said.

"How much are we talking?" Jackson asked.

Andreas looked at him. "Jesus boy, are you a professional wrestler?" he asked.

Jackson laughed.

"Twenty thousand," Andreas said.

"Also, and I'm sorry I forgot to mention this, but we're going to need a ride back a week later," I said.

Andreas looked at me again and rubbed his white beard.

"It happens to be that our cruise is only a few days. We should be able to do that, but it'll be another ten grand. I'm sorry, but believe it or not, these flat earthers don't have a lot of money and every little bit helps. We can drop you off and pick you up a week later," Andreas said.

"That's perfect," I said.

"Here's a check for 60. Double what you need. Can you get us down there in 1 day instead? Jean asked as he handed it over to him.

Andreas looked over the check and smiled. "I'll see what I can do. For now, go bunk up. Max will show you where everything is. Try to enjoy yourself for a change Graham, you look stressed," Andreas said and turned around.

Max's eyes bugged out as he led us out and down into where all the rooms were. He set us up in a big suite for all of us, which is how we travel best anyway.

"OK guys, I'll be back in two hours to get you. You're going to love this," Max said as he left.

I looked at everybody. "So does that mean that Max and his dad are flat earthers?" I asked.

"I think they just are businessmen with a boat," Josh said.

"You know we're going to have to interact with other people eventually, right?" Rosette asked.

"Why can't we just hide in the room?" Jackson asked.

"Because that's not right. Let's try to have fun for once in our lives," Hannah said.

They're never going to come back for you. They're going to leave you for dead in that ice mountain. They'll never find your bodies, you stupid dumbass!

I went to the bathroom to take a leak. I looked at myself in the mirror. I was completely convinced at that moment that hell is a real place and it's on earth. But I was in for the surprise of my lifetime.

The hardest thing to explain is the glaringly evident which everybody had decided not to see—Ayn Rand

Chapter Twenty-Four

I came out of the room and found everybody sitting with some new friends. I came to the lounge chairs they were lying on and made myself at home. It was strange being on a small cruise boat while everybody was wearing winter get ups, but it is what it is. Beggars can't be choosers. I turned my attention to this young person who was talking to my friends and wife.

"The thing you have to understand about globeheads is that they don't understand that we have science behind us. It's really hard to find any evidence for a flat stationary earth. Nearly every single point made by a flat earther can be explained with basic physics. At the end of the day, a lot of flat earthers retreat to their comfort zone and wave off any explanation they don't understand," this kid began.

"The problem is that physics is based on a series of false premises. Gravity waves and black holes are nonsense, but necessary for the math to work," another person said.

I looked over to Jackson and smiled. I saw that the vein in his neck was bulging and so were the veins on his biceps. I know he was dying to jump in.

"I'm going to go to the bar and grab myself a drink," Jackson said, as he stood up quickly and shuffled away.

Globeheads. I never heard that term before.

"Think in terms of Occam's Razor. You know the presupposition that the simplest explanation is usually the correct one? Is it even possible to be an eight thousand mile diameter ball, comprised of 71% water (water can only be held in a container), spinning one thousand and forty miles at the 'equator' while hurling around the "sun" at sixty six thousand miles per hour, which moves five hundred thousand miles per hour in the "Milky Way," while it moves two million miles per hour. Yet, every day or night, Polaris remains above the north pole, and the constellations remain in the same spot. To date, no one has drilled deeper than eight miles into the earth, so NO ONE has any idea, factually what lies beneath. You can research things like Operation Highjump, and Operation Fishbowl," another one said.

Now my blood in my veins was starting to boil. I wanted to educate them about the precision of the equinox and of the Zodiac, the twelve signs and everything that I know. I decided to follow suit and find Jackson.

I excused myself and walked towards the bar where I found Jackson chugging a beer.

"This place makes me want to drink 12 of these," he said pointing to his beer, "then rip my shirt off, go back there, flip the chairs over and start throwing them into the water one by one," he said.

"Calm down Jax, they're harmless," I said.

"Then why are you here right now?" he asked.

"Yeah you got a point. Tender, let me get one of those," I said as he handed me a beer.

We clinked beers and drank.

"They started talking about stars and constellations being stationary, though we are hurtling through space," I said.

Jackson almost spit his beer out at me and laughed. "So that's what got you. I wonder what they're going to say to piss Rosette or Larisa off," he asked.

We finished our beers, and Jackson started walking back. I turned to the bartender and ordered 2 quick shots and 2 more beers. I took the shots of Patron to the face, and then cracked the two beers and caught up with Jackson.

"One for the road?" I asked.

"I'm good man, give it to your wife," he said.

I handed Hannah the beer and she looked at me and smiled. I sat down. I hadn't eaten in a while and I developed a baby buzz. The trick was to not binge out and just ride this out, which I wasn't so good at.

"So what have you guys been talking about since I left?" Jackson asked.

"We can't feel our motion through space, nor has any physical experiment ever proved that the Earth actually is in motion. That's Lincoln Barrett, a historian," one person said.

"The failure of the many attempts to measure terrestrially any effects of the earth's motion. That's physicist Wolfgang Pauli," another person said.

"Thus, even now, three and a half centuries after Galileo, it is still remarkably difficult to say categorically whether the Earth moves. Physicist Julian B. Barbour. Also, Physicist I. Bernard Cohen says, 'There is no planetary observation by which we on Earth can prove that the Earth is moving in an orbit around the Sun,' " the first person said.

"Don't you ever wonder why they don't make movies about the Flat Earth conspiracy? Tons of space alien movies and everything else but no Flat Earth movies," another person said.

"1 Chronicles 16:30 'Tremble before him, all the earth. The world also is established that it can't be moved.' The kid who started about the constellations said to me. I feel like he was trolling me at this point."

"Honestly speaking, the easiest way to understand the world being fact without the headache of doing so much work is to understand the Bible. Once you begin to realize the men who created our modern day science all worshipped Lucifer, it was all designed to discredit and shun God and what HE says. That it's immovable. We're in a dome and he sits above us. Then it just makes so much sense that the world is flat. When you go deep in the spiritual aspect of flat earth. The men created our science to eventually get us to believe in aliens, that's the last card for the NWO one world religion. Joshua 10:13 mentions the Sun standing still for twenty-four hours. Doesn't mention the earth rotating. Remember that," he said.

This was the part of the conversation where I would call Blur up and have this guy on. But first I wanted to correct him that Lucifer is not the Devil and school him on Astronomy and Astrology. Then again, if Jackson can bite his tongue, I should be able to as well.

"What about the Qu'ran? Surah Al-Kahf (18:47) And remember the Day we shall cause the mountains to pass away like clouds of dust, and you will see the Earth as a leveled plain, and we shall gather them all together so as to leave not one of them behind. Surah Yunus (10:5), he it is who gave the Sun radiance and the Moon light, and determined the stages (for the waxing and waning of the

Moon) that you may learn the calculations of years and the reckoning of time. Allah has created all this with a rightful purpose. "He expounds his signs for the people who know," another person said.

I thought about that last quote, he expounds his signs for the people who know. The twelve signs. Judaism and Christianity were anthropomorphic allegorical, meta-phorical stories about the sun and the zodiac and the constellations. Why wouldn't Islam be as well? I hadn't studied it much, nor had I really thought about it since I learned about Alberto Rivera a while back. I wasn't sure if that was real still, maybe I'd never know. I felt my buzz starting to dwindle and motioned for Rosette to come with me. She stood up and we walked towards the bar.

"How are you feeling Newsdon?" she asked as I ordered another beer and a shot.

"Not that good. It's pretty hard to keep it under control. These drinks are the only things that seem to calm me down," I said.

"The second we get home, that same day, you need to make an appointment with a psychiatrist. I mean it. I'll have you committed if you don't take care of this that day. I'm so worried about you Graham," she said.

I gave her a hug and promised her that I would take care of it. She walked back to everyone. I took another shot at the bar and left the bartender a twenty. My buzz was coming back. The voice seems to leave me alone more when I have more to drink. I walked back to where everybody was sitting.

"It's simple really, God created the earth on the first day and he created the sun on the fourth day. How does that work on a heliocentric model?" my troller asked.

"Psalm 93:1 'Thou hast fixed the Earth immovable and firm.' I mean, what more do you need?" he continued.

"When do the sun and the moon sit still?" Hannah asked.

"Joshua 10:12-13 Then spake Joshua to the Lord in the day when the Lord delivered up the Amorites before the children of Israel, and he said in the sight of Israel, Sun stand thou still upon Gibeon; and thou, Moon, in the valley of Ayalon. And the sun stood still in the midst of heaven, and hastened not to go down about a whole day. The Sun and the Moon were commanded to stand still, not the earth," he said.

"I know it was said, but it's simple. What is pushing us through space hundreds of thousands of miles per hour? Shouldn't eventually our momentum start to slow down? If we are spinning around a star that's spinning around a galaxy that's swirling around the universe, why do the stars stay relatively in the same position for thousands of years?" a young boy said.

I never thought much about Flat Earther's. I didn't know they had words like Globetards and Globies. Blur never talks about it. It must be the only conspiracy he refuses to touch. What surprised me the most was how religious many of them were. It has been so long since I've read the Bible for its original intended purposes but I forgot about the flat Earth quotes. These people seemed nice and have seem to have built up quite a repertoire of things to guide their point of view. I know that Jackson is dying to explain to them that snipers have to account for the curvature of the Earth's rotation in order to take out their target, among a hundred things. This guy built his life around his love of Physics, and working out. This must have been killing him.

"Alright guys. It's 9 o'clock. Let's go to the club inside," Max said.

I hadn't noticed that he was back, but I would do anything for some loud music, some drinks and to get away from these conversations. Also, when I listen to music, I don't have any way to hear the voices. It's kind of hard to explain.

We made our way inside to a nice playlist of house music. Man, if there was one person I could bring back to life for one more show, it would definitely be Avicii. I saw Max walking up to me at the bar. I ordered two more shots and another beer. My buzz was getting stronger.

"Hey Graham, did you know that EW Bullinger in the late 19th century wrote a book called Witness of the Stars where he tried to make the case that the zodiac and the constellations can make a legitimate case for Christ?" he asked.

I looked at him and smiled and handed him a shot. We clinked and took it together.

"Did you know that the Bible at the time only knew about 48 constellations and we're up to 88 now?" I asked.

"But did you know about Bullinger?" he asked.

I shook my head. "I'll have to look into it," I said.

"Genesis 1:14, 'Then God said 'let there be lights in the firmament of the heavens to divide the day from the night; and let them be for signs and seasons for days and years,' " he said and smiled.

This kid has watched my stuff. I also don't remember that verse. One of these days I'm going to have to read the Bible cover to cover and decode the entire thing.

"Also, in the Living Bible, Job 9:9 'He made the Bear, Orion and the Pleiades, and the constellations of the southern Zodiac,' " he said.

"What do you believe in Max?" I turned and asked him.

"I believe what you believe in. I've been doing my own research. I've outlined some of Islam and found that it's the same stuff. Can I send you what I have?" he asked.

"Sure," I said as I gave him my email address.

"Did you also know that in India they worshipped the Cow or the Bull? That's where the phrase Holy Cow comes in. Also, look at this picture I found. Islamic writing showing Aquarius and Pisces," he said.

"Definitely interesting," I said. I wasn't very familiar with Islam. I looked at my beer, and took one last sip and put it on the counter. My buzz was seriously strong, I was done. I had things to do in the morning.

I walked over to where my friends were and told them that I was going to bed. They said they would meet back in the suite later, they were going to stay out. I walked back to my room with Max who was seriously chatty the entire time. He finally said goodnight after about a half an hour and after we took a few pictures together. I lay down in my bed, slightly dizzy. I closed my eyes. Right before I fell asleep, I heard a creepy message.

If they don't come back for you, you'll die with your treasure. You don't even know what you're walking into.

All truths are easy to understand once they are dis-covered; the point is to discover them—Galileo Galilei

Chapter Twenty-Five

I woke up with a killer hangover. I opened my eyes, and I was holding Hannah like a snuggle pillow. My hand was on her belly. Maybe what she went through was affecting me more than I like to admit. I stood up and lit a cigarette. I held it in for a few seconds to really feel the nicotine then blew it out. I put on my pants and went to the bar to get a glass of orange juice or Gatorade, whatever they had. It was chilly outside, which felt good against my skin. I get too uncomfortable in the heat. I went to the bartender and he took one look at me and handed me a frozen bottle of Poland Spring and two Motrin. I thanked him and flicked my cigarette over the side of the boat. I popped the Motrin and pounded the water. I made my way back to the suite where everybody was still asleep. I climbed back in bed with Hannah and gave her a kiss on the cheek. She smiled and opened her eyes and turned around to face me.

"I know what you're going through baby," she said.

I stared at her.

"Rosette got drunk last night and told me everything," she said.

Damn it, Rosette.

"Why did you think you couldn't tell me?" she asked.

"Because with the miscarriage and the torture, honestly I didn't want to worry you," Graham said.

"I know that you're drinking more because it helps make it go away. To be honest, I don't know what you're going through or how you function with that going on. Can you hear them right now?" she asked worried.

I nodded.

"What are they saying?" she asked.

"You're going to die," I said.

She looked at me and then adjusted her bra and then gave me a big hug. I mean she really squeezed the hell out of me.

"I know we will get through this together sweetie. Think of everything we've been through. I'm not going to lose you to this," she said.

I nodded.

"Do you ever get the urge to listen to the voice?" she asked.

"Hell no, but still it's hard to focus and function," I said.

"What are you two talking about?" Rosette asked as she woke up and yawned.

"What do you think we're talking about?" I asked her.

"I thought I dreamed that conversation. Graham, I'm so sorry, but I was dying on the inside. I had to tell your wife. It just wasn't fair. You're not alone in this," she said.

"Thank you, Rosette. But PLEASE don't tell anybody else," I said.

She nodded.

We let everyone sleep as Rosette, Hannah and I went downstairs to get breakfast. We loaded up on carbs. Rosette had brought a backpack with her and filled it up with bagels and jelly and food that we could take with us to the mountain. Just as we wrapped up breakfast, Max found us again.

"Hey guys," he said.

"What's going on Max?" I asked.

"Nothing much Graham. Hey, you guys need to get ready because we are going to drop you off in an hour," he said.

We looked at him. For about thirty-six hours, I had forgotten that we actually had something to do. Once we get back to the States, I'm going to set us up on a cruise together.

"Thanks, Max, we'll meet you by the front of the boat in an hour," I said as I motioned for Hannah and Rosette to follow me.

We walked back to our suite on the boat. When we got there, we found that everybody was rotating taking showers and packing their things up.

"Baby, do you want to shower together to save some time?" Hannah looked over to me.

"That will NOT save time. And I'm not getting into a sticky shower, thank you," Rosette said.

I laughed.

After about half an hour, we were all ready to go. We put our bags on our backs and went to the front of the boat where we met the Captain and his son again.

"Well Graham, I trust that you and your friends had a good time here?" Andreas asked.

"We certainly did, thank you," I said.

"Are you Flat Earth convinced?" Max smiled.

"You're not a flat Earther are you?" I asked.

"No, but it's amazing the kinds of things people believe in these days with all their 'secret information,'" he said.

"Here we are. You guys get off here. This is as close as we can get. We'll be here same time one week from today. If you're not here, we're going to have to leave you, I'm sorry," Andreas said.

I snapped a picture of where we were for posterity.

"Alright guys take care," Max said as he waved us off.

"Tell everyone it was nice meeting them for us," Josh said.

"Will do. Thanks," Max said.

They made their way through the icy water and dropped us off at the edge of that mountain. We might be able to make it in one day and not even need the tent. We would need to start a fire too. Lucky for me I had a Dragon Laser on me, which is basically a laser pointer that can start a fire. We were almost there, we just needed to survive the mountain.

All things are possible. Who you are is limited by who you think you are—Egyptian Book of the Dead

Chapter Twenty-Six

We made our way to the mountain. It took us three hours just to get to the base of it.

"OK guys are you ready for this?" I asked as I shook off another mean tweet from the voice in my head.

"Exactly what are we looking for?" Josh asked.

"I'm not entirely sure, but I think we'll know when we see it," I said.

I hope I was right.

We started climbing the mountain. It was a long daunting and arduous task. After about two hours, we took a break to set up shop.

"I didn't realize how exhausting this was going to be, and I swam for my college money," Rosette said.

"Yeah, this is more intense than any interval training I've ever been a part of," Jackson said.

"Guys, we have to keep going," I said.

"Hold up guys I'll be right back," I said.

I walked over to the side where something caught my eye. When I reached it, I was shocked at what I saw.

It was a dead body, very fresh from the looks of it, though the deep freeze of the Antarctic could be playing tricks on us. I went through his pockets and found a Geophone. I turned it on and surprisingly it still worked. Well, now we had a communication device here, maybe Larisa could hack it. I took off his backpack and brought it back with me.

"Hey guys, look what I found," I said.

"Was that a dead body?" Hannah asked.

"Yes it was. Whatever he was looking for he didn't find it unfortunately," I said.

"Hey Graham, you're going to want to see this," Jackson said.

He had opened the backpack and emptied the contents out. There was freeze dried food and an ominous letter. I read it over. I looked at Josh and handed it to him.

He scanned the letter with his eyes a few times.

"What does it say?" Rosette asked.

"The mountain shall receive you," Josh said.

"Well, that's not bad," Hannah said.

"No, you don't understand. It comes from a Gnostic gospel, damn it. I forget which one. There's a story about people running and hiding and praying to God, and the mountain opened up and swallowed them and protected them. We're probably looking for a set of doors or

217

something, or a pathway into the mountain. That could be impossible based on the size of this freaking thing," Josh said.

"Oh, and it's signed with the hieroglyphs that make up the word Osirica as well," I said.

"I didn't even notice that, but you're right," Josh said to me.

"So they ended up sending someone. Larisa, can you take a look at this phone and see if there's some way to make it useful for us?" I asked.

"Sure thing Graham. Can we camp here for the night?" Hannah asked.

"I want to walk a little more and then we'll rest for the night," I said.

We started walking up the mountain again as Larisa fiddled with our new toy.

We got to a point of flat plain and I stopped.

"Who has the zoom lens thingy?" I asked.

"I do. Why? Do you want it?" Larisa asked.

I nodded.

"OK, here you go," she said.

I looked through them up the mountain from where I was standing looking for something that would allow me to believe we weren't on a suicide mission. About halfway up I saw what looked like two giant steel doors.

"Hey Jackson, check this out," I said as I handed him the mini scope. I guided it over to where I wanted him to look.

"Wow Graham.This has to be it," he said.

"I was thinking the same thing," I said.

"I want to see," Hannah said.

Jackson handed her the scope, and she looked. One by one the remaining team looked and saw what I saw.

"We can keep going now or we can rest for the night. I figure we could get up there in a few more hours," I said.

"Too tired, need sleep," Rosette said.

"Alright, let's mark our territory."

We unpacked the tent from Jackson's enormous back. He and I set it up while everyone else started pulling food and drinks out of their bags.

"I don't suppose one of you brought a bottle of liquor with you, did you?" I asked jokingly.

Everyone stared at me. Apparently that was not funny.

"I was just kidding guys," I said.

"We never know with you," Hannah said.

We got in the tent and passed out fruit and bread. Considering we were in the Antarctic, there was surprisingly little wind. We were actually pretty warm in there.

It wasn't our normal travel accommodations, but it would do.

"Hey Graham, I think I figured it out. This thing is a live phone, with GPS capabilities. We got a few text messages since we started walking again," Larisa said.

"Well, what does it say?" I asked.

It's good to see you're moving again. We assumed you had died. We see you stopped again, we're assuming for the night. When do you believe you will have secured the location so we can send an extraction team and destroy the Library. It's too visible now. We will have to give the Vatican the Q-Document, but aside from that we will burn the rest down – P.

"Holy crap guys!" Rosette said.

"What's the Q-Document?" Jackson asked.

"It's a rumored document that exists that nobody has ever been able to prove. It's the literal words of Jesus Christ," Josh said.

"I'm confused. I thought Jesus wasn't real," Hannah asked.

"He wasn't, this is a control mechanism. This has to be their end game, to release this to the Vatican so they can release it and 'prove' existence," I said.

"What should I say back?" Larisa asked.

"Let them know you're safe, and you'll be there in a day and a half. Once you locate and secure the document, you will let them know."

"OK done. Who's P?" she asked.

"It's got to be the Pindar," I replied.

Everybody looked at me.

"Well who else would it be?" I asked.

"Alright guys let's get some sleep. We have a big day tomorrow," Rosette said.

"Agreed," Jackson said as he rolled over.

We rolled over and tried to fall asleep. Believe it or not, our body heat was generating a decent amount of heat. We had to open the tent flap to get some non-existent wind in here. Our tent slowly cooled down and we fell fast asleep not knowing what would wake us up violently in the morning.

Those who are able to see beyond the shadows and lies of their culture will never be understood, let alone believed, by the masses—Plato

Chapter Twenty-Seven

"WAKE UP!!!"

Someone was tapping on our tent with what looked like an AR-15. It took me a minute to wipe the sleep from my eyes before we all got up and unzipped the tent. It was two people brandishing guns.

"Who are you? What are you doing here? You're not supposed to be here," one of the men said.

"Hold on a minute. Slow down. Just put the guns down and we'll tell you," I said.

The men looked at each other and pointed their guns at us.

"Okay, we'll do it your way. My name is Graham. This is Hannah, my wife, Rosette, Jean, Larisa and Josh," I said.

"What is that supposed to mean?" the second man said. The second man had a pronounced Spanish accent.

"Look, we are looking for something important, it's imperative that we make our way to that ridge on the mountain right there," Josh said.

The men looked up, squinting against the Sun.

"What do you want up there?" the first man asked.

"There is something up there that is incredibly important. Please allow us to continue. Who are you anyway?" I asked.

"We are the scientists that work in those red buildings down there," the second man said.

"You're the Chilean scientists?" Rosette asked.

They nodded.

"OK look, we are not here to cause any trouble. You can come with us up the mountain if you'd like to see what's there," I said.

The men looked at each other and shook their heads and pointed the guns back at us.

"Please, you don't understand. There is something incredibly important up there. We're going up there with or without you. You're just going to have to shoot me in the back then," I said as I turned around and took two steps and extended my arms out like a crucifix.

"Stop walking," the first man said.

I turned around and looked at everyone and realized that Jackson wasn't with us. Out of the corner of my eye I saw him in the tent trying to unzip it from the back. I just had to create a diversion.

"Why don't you just come with us. You obviously don't want to shoot us, or you would have already. Please, nobody will have to know a thing," I said.

They looked at each other and both trained their guns at me.

Suddenly Jackson came from behind them and knocked their heads together. Like, straight out of a Dwayne Johnson movie. They both fell on the floor, unconscious.

"Thanks Jax," I said.

"No prob Graham. What are we going to do with them?" he asked.

"I'm not really sure. We can't carry them back to their base. It's too cold to leave them outside, and, if given the chance, they'd probably call their government, and we'd be swarmed in no time. There's an Antarctic Treaty System on these lands remember," I said.

"Why don't we put them in the tent?" Rosette asked.

We looked over at her. "That's not a bad idea," Hannah said.

"What's the point of that? They'd just leave," Jean said.

"Not if I lock the tent closed," Larisa said.

With that, she went in the tent and opened up her purse. She had two small locks that I swear she uses for her diaries. What's with these mini locks everywhere?

"We'll lock the tent closed," she said.

"Then what? We'll go up the mountain and if something is there, we're there for a week. Then we come back down and they're dead," Rosette said.

"Not if we leave them a bag of food," Larisa said.

We looked at her. If all goes well, we will be here for four to five days and then have to head back to hitch a ride with the flatties. They're not the only ones that can come up with nicknames.

"Won't they just tear the tent apart?" Jackson asked.

"Check them for anything sharp. Check the tent for anything sharp. This could actually work," I said as I picked up the two guns and handed them over to Jackson. God if they ever make a black Rambo, he needs to be it.

Jackson cleared the tent and patted these two down. He took a pen from one of their pockets and then picked them both up at the same time and placed them in the tent. Larisa then locked the zippers together on both sides and we were on our way.

"What's the first book you want to see if this exists?" Jackson asked.

"I want to see this Q-Document," I said.

Truth was, there was so many other books that could be in there. Five days was not going to be enough.

We trekked up the mountain until we finally reached the ledge. Once we got there, we knew we were onto something. This was a giant stone that was split in half. There was a sensor on it.

"Larisa!" I said.

"Just a sec," she said as she pulled out her master thumbprint. She pressed it to the sensor, and it beeped green. Suddenly, these two massive doors opened.

"But Elizabeth, when she heard that they sought for John, took him and went up into the hill-country and looked about her where she should hide him; and there was no hiding place. And Elizabeth groaned and said with a loud voice: O mountain of God, receive thou a mother with a child. For Elizabeth was not able to go up. And immediately the mountain clave asunder and took her in. And there was a light shining a way for them: for an angel of the Lord was with them, keeping watch over them," Josh said.

"What's that?" I asked.

"That's the verse I couldn't remember earlier. It's from the Infancy Gospel of James," Josh said.

We started walking inside and looked up. There was a giant inscription.

Those who seek should not stop seeking until they find.

Josh turned to us, "The Gospel of Thomas."

226

We started walking inside and it gradually became darker. Then I noticed there were candles strategically placed an inch away from each other. There must have been thousands and thousands of these. I took out the laser pointer and aimed it at one of the candles. It ignited, and then started to catch all the way down. The place lit up. Once it did, we were shook.

This was the largest library I had ever seen. Words cannot describe just how many books there were before us. Rows and rows of beautiful books. I actually got teary eyed over this. I walked up to the first section and looked at the books they had.

Aristarchus of Samos Astronomy book. This one outlined heliocentrism and was a lost work.

Aristotle's second book of Poetics

Protrepticus

Julius Caesar De Astris Liber

Callinicus to Cleopatra, on the History of Alexan-dria

Eratosthenes on the measurement of Earth

Eratosthenes Georgraphica

Eudemus History of Arithmetics

Eudemus History of Astronomy

Pliny the Elder History of his times.

Poems from Pliny the Younger

Astronomy works of Apuleius

Works by Porphyry 'Against the Christians'

Book of Vai Ze. Guide to the forms and habits of all 11,520 types of supernatural creatures in the world and how to overcome their hauntings and attacks, to the Yellow Emperor in the twenty sixth century BC

Priceless, absolutely priceless, but this wasn't going to help me in what I needed to do. I kept looking around.

"Hey Graham, you're going to want to see this," Jackson said.

I walked over to the other side where Jackson was and looked. This was exactly what I was looking for. I started to shake.

The Book of the Covenant from Exodus 24:7
The Book of the Wars of the Lord Numbers 21:14
Book of Nathan the Prophet
History of Nathan the Prophet
The Gospel of Eve
The Book of Jasher
The Protevangelion
The Gospel of the Infancy of Jesus Christ
The Infancy Gospel of Thomas
The Epistles of Jesus Christ and Abgarus
The Gospel of Nicodemus
The Apostles Creed
The Epistle of Paul the Apostle to the Laodiceans

The Gospel of the Four Heavenly Realms
Complete works of Hypatia.

I was going to need everyone's help going through this. This was the goldmine.

"Hey someone toss me that phone we found," I said.

The phone came flying my way.

I picked it up and dialed Dexter.

"Hi Dexter, it's Graham. I have that ending you were looking for," I said as I hung up the phone.

"Hey guys, this place has WiFi," Larisa said.

"How is that even possible?" Jackson asked.

"I don't know, but I cracked it. I wormed into my computer and I sent the man we were talking to our coordinates. He said 'You are owed a debt of gratitude, we'll be there in two days.' " Larisa said.

I cracked the first book.

In the beginning....

Know thyself—Socrates

Chapter Twenty-Eight

Fifteen days later

We were back home. It was a long two weeks. The men who maintain the balance came with food and let us stay an additional week. Unbelievable. Also, they spoke to those men in the tent, and they basically left us alone. I have no idea what they said to them, but I was grateful I didn't have to deal with them anymore. I was able to outline the entire Bible and find all the correlations to the stars and the signs. I felt like my work was complete. Venus Lair would have their story wrapped up completely and begin pushing it asap. I finally felt like I had really accomplished something in my life.

"Alright Newsdon, it's time," Rosette said.

"What do you mean?" I asked.

"You're taking the Minnesota test," she said.

"Nothing about Minnesota!" I yelled back.

"I'm sorry, that's an unfortunate coincidence, but you promised you'd take it," Rosette said.

"Alright, what do I need to do for it?" I asked.

"Just bring a pencil," she said.

Who has pencils anymore. I scurried across my room looking for a pencil and finally found half of one with the eraser chewed off. It may have been in the family since Clinton was in office.

"Be truthful Graham. There are failsafes built into this test, so I'll know if you're lying," Rosette said.

I hadn't planned on lying, but some of those questions were unbelievably personal.

Two hours later, I emerged and went to the couch. This test took the life out of me. I cracked a beer.

Once this movie goes viral, you're going to have religious people across the country out to kill you. I hope you can live with that. You put your wife and friends in jeopardy.

God, how long would it take to get results. I'm not even sure what she's looking for.

After about two hours Rosette came out of the room looking sad.

"What is it Rose?" I asked.

"Graham, sit down for a minute," she said.

"You're making me nervous," I said.

"The first thing you need to understand is that we're here for you. We will ALWAYS be here for you," she said.

"What is it?" I asked, starting to lose patience.

"The second scale spiked on this test. I would venture to say that you are clinically depressed," she said.

"Well, I've had a lot of things go on in my life the last few years Rose. I mean come on, you have to give me that," I said.

"Also, the sixth scale peaked a bit. You have trust issues. This was the paranoia scale. It shows that you've been degrading over time, at least from what I remember of you up to now," she said. "Here's the big one," she said.

"What?" I asked.

"The Schizophrenia scale came back negative," she said.

"That's a good thing, right?" I asked.

"It is. But the mania scale came back through the roof. I'm not a psychiatrist yet Graham, but this has every indication that you are bipolar," she said.

"I'm what? No, I'm just depressed because of what I've gone through," I said.

"You have delusions of grandeur ever since you were a teenager. Always thought you were going to change the world, always thought that you were the only one who understood what you did," she said.

"Look at what I've, no what we've accomplished. We're having a movie made about our adventure for Christ sake," I said.

"The voices Graham—bipolar, schizophrenia, borderline personality disorder— they all manifest in your early twenties. Your struggles with alcohol. How you drink ALL THE TIME. It's not just a weekend or one day a week thing with you. Everybody's noticed. The way you microdose all the time. Also, your voices are violent and we're all pretty scared for you," Rosette said.

"I know you're worried, but I'm going to get help, I told you I would," I said.

"That's not good enough honey," Hannah said.

"What?" I asked.

"I've let a lot go when it comes to you. I know we've been through everything and will continue to. I know you're going to hate me for this," Hannah said.

"Hate you for what?" I asked.

Just then two men in white scrubs wearing gloves came up the stairs to our house.

"You did not call them!" I yelled at Hannah.

"I'm sorry baby, but I love you enough to be willing to lose you this way, but I won't lose you another way. You are not in control of yourself and you need all the help you get. These two are from Pembroke and they will take good care of you," Hannah said.

"The mental hospital? You can't be serious?" I asked.

"I'm sorry Newsdon, it's the only way," Rosette said.

"Shut up Rosette. This is all your fault. If you hadn't given me that test," I said.

Rosette looked at me.

"I know you don't mean that," she said as she turned away from me.

I looked at the situation and assessed it.

"Graham baby, please go with them or they are going to call the police," Hannah said.

I have never felt such anger at people I love and such an incredible sadness at the same time. I was completely defeated. I was so angry at the moment that it never occurred to me that they were right and that I did need some serious help.

I walked into my room and packed a duffle bag of clothes. I came out and started walking with the men.

"Just one minute," one of the men said as he opened my bag.

"What are you doing?" I asked.

"I have to check it for weapons or anything that can harm you," the man said.

"You're kidding. You think I'm going to kill myself? Or someone else?" I asked incredulously.

"It's in our job description," the man said.

"Baby, you have a voice in your head that threatens to kill you," Hannah said starting to cry.

It was at that moment, when I saw how much I was hurting her, that my heart sank. She was the love of my life and she had done everything for me always. This time around I was tested more than before, but I decided at that moment to leave without a problem.

"Also, please take your shoelaces and hoodie string out," the second man said.

"Seriously?" I asked as I looked to them.

They were serious.

"Fine," I said as I took them both out.

I did the walk of shame past everybody in the living room and to the back stairs.

"We'll be here when you get out Graham," Jackson said.

I couldn't even bring myself to look at them. I just walked down the stairs, and, once I got downstairs, they made me get on a gurney and strapped me down. I'd never been so humiliated in my life.

Chapter Twenty-Nine

One week later

"So Graham, when did the depression start?" the Doctor asked me.

I sat back in the chair and took a look at him. For the last week I had been pretty uncooperative, and it wasn't getting me anywhere. They had started me on Lithium and Zoloft. I could feel something happening, but it wasn't fully working yet. The Zoloft was giving me endless diarrhea. I thought about my friends and wife at home and realized that, if I wanted to get out of this place, I was going to have to play by their rules.

"I suppose it started when my dad died," I said.

"Really? Tell me more about it," the doctor said.

"He was a newsman, an editor and producer for the local news channel. One day when I was 10, he came home from work and we were all sitting down for dinner, and he just fell forward into his plate. By the time the paramedics got there, he was gone," I said.

"And you were at the dinner table?" he asked.

"Me, my brother James and my mom. James dove into school and eventually joined the Marines. I dove into work and decided to become a doctor so that if I was in a situation like that again I would know what to do and be able to help. My mom, she never recovered though. She started drinking shortly afterwards," I said.

"I see. From what I know, your father had an undiagnosed congenital heart issue and there was nothing that could be done about it," the doctor said.

I nodded.

"It must have been incredibly traumatizing for you. Have you accepted that what happened to your father was not your fault?" the doctor asked me.

I looked at him and then looked down at the floor.

"There was nothing that could have been done. Your brother was too busy with his own life to take care of you. You looked for a male role model, but nobody could fill the void. That's why you are so close to your male friends. You treat your friends like family, because the truth is, they are your family. You're still incredibly hurt that they put you here, but can you understand that it is for your own good?" the doctor asked.

I looked away.

"As far as your mother goes, that was the love of her life. She never remarried, hardly dated from what you've told me over the last week. She kept to herself and the bottle. He was to her what Hannah is to you. Do you think that you picked up the bottle in a way to feel closer to her?" the doctor asked.

Wow! Exactly what Rosette said to me.

"I have considered it Doc, but the thing is that when I have some drinks and get a buzz on, it takes away the anxiety and the nerves. I feel free for a short time," I said.

"I know Graham. It's typical with people with ADHD, bipolar, schizophrenia or borderline personality disorder to abuse things like pills and alcohol. It's an escape. That's what the medicine you're on now will do for you. I see so many patients, once their medicine has fully reached their system, they have no need for distractions like you. You've been undiagnosed since you were a child, and you were self-medicating the whole time without knowing that was what you were doing. Believe it or not, I see real progress in you. You've been here a week and haven't mentioned having a drink once to anyone," the doctor said.

I looked at the doctor. I hadn't thought about that. My thoughts were starting to clear a little. The voice was still there, but it was fading. I don't understand why some people have voices that are friendly and some that are angry. They are both equally dangerous.

"Tell me Graham, you don't like me very much do you?" the doctor asked.

I stared blankly at him.

"It's alright. I'm not here to make friends, I'm here to fix things," he said as he looked at his watch. "Alright, it's time for your medicine. Go to the window, you know the drill," he said as he closed his laptop where he was taking notes.

I stood up and went out of the room I was in. I went to the window and washed down the medicine. There was a payphone at the end of the hall where Hannah and my friends would call, and I could talk to them. I'm sure it was monitored, but it is what it is. They don't even let you have razors here, only electric ones, and that doesn't really work for my face, so I've been growing a beard. I haven't had a beard since Rosette slapped the ever-loving life out of me after NP died. For most people it enhances their face, but I look like a completely different person. I was liking it though. The payphone started to ring, and I sat down on the chair in the hall and started watching some TV. After a few, I was bored and went into the closet to look for a book to read. I found a tattered book, the only novel in there called 'The Blood of the Lamb'. I flipped to the back page. It was about the Vatican extracting DNA from the Shroud of Turin to clone Jesus with unintended consequences. I laughed, knowing what I know, but figured I'd give it a chance. The news was on TV. Then something unexpected happened.

We're just getting confirmed reports right now that Graham Newsdon, the Quincy local with controversial, eccentric views on religion who has been a staple around the theaters in Boston for his lectures, has checked into rehab voluntarily to battle an unknown addiction. This news channel has reached out to his wife, and she has provided no comment on this. More as the story develops.

I sat in my chair. Who leaked this? How did these people know so much? Where did my privacy go?

"Hey Graham, you have a call," one of the orderlies said.

I stood up and walked to the phone in the back of the room.

"Hi baby," Hannah said.

"Did you see the news?" I asked.

"Yeah Rosette just told me about it. The Zip Code Bandits figured this out. I don't know how. None of us leaked anything," she said.

"Well that's great. Now I have to dye my hair, get glasses and grow a beard," I said.

"No you don't sweetie, although, I do like you with a beard," she said.

"So what's going on Hannah?" I asked.

I could hear her voice starting to crack.

"Nothing. I just wanted to check in with you and see how you were doing. I'm told that the medicine is starting to work. Is that true?" she asked.

"You could say that. I think it just needs some time," I said.

Hannah was quiet for a second. "The check from the movie studio came in today. You didn't tell me it was going to be so much," she said trying to change the topic to something happier.

"Yeah, sorry. It's been a crazy few weeks with everything that happened. Put it in our joint, and when it clears pay off the mortgage," I said.

"I already did," Hannah said.

"Good," I said.

"Hold on a sec. Someone wants to say hello to you," Hannah said as I heard her pass the phone.

"Hi Newsdon. How are you feeling?" Rosette asked.

"I'm doing better honestly," I said.

"So does that mean you're not mad at me anymore?" she asked.

I thought about it for a second. I was on a self-destructive path, and if I didn't get a kick in the ass when I did, I might not have made it to this point.

"We're cool sweetie," I said.

"Oh thank God. I'm so happy. Hold on here's your wife," she said as I heard the phone pass back.

"I'm going to come visit you tomorrow sweetie. Is there anything you want me to bring?" Hannah asked.

"Food, lots of it. It sucks here. I must have lost 10 pounds already," I said.

"You got it sweetie," She said. "I love you baby."

"Love you too. See you tomorrow," I said.

3 weeks later

"So Graham, tell me how you feel. Are the voices still here?" the doctor asked.

"They're gone. I haven't heard them in almost a month," I said.

"That's wonderful news. How's your mood?" he asked.

"To be honest, I feel like the medicine is working. I've been mentally at peace for the last two weeks," I said.

"That's terrific. Do you have any urge to drink, or micro dose?" he asked.

"To be honest, no. My mind is calm, and my depression seems to be gone," I said.

"That's so great to hear. You will always have anxiety, but you'll find that it will be manageable instead of crippling. I'm so glad to hear how you're doing. If we release you, what are you going to do?" he asked.

"Well first, I'm going to go home and have sex with my wife," I said.

The doctor laughed.

"Second, I'm going to keep writing. I feel like I've found something that really helps me in a positive way," I said.

"You're still smoking cigarettes?" he asked.

I nodded.

"I shouldn't be saying this but, in the grand scheme of things, that's not a bad way of coping. I hope you quit one day, but it's fine for now," the doctor said.

"So, what now Doctor?" I asked.

"Now we give you another week or two of monitoring, and then we release you with bottles of pills and send you on your way," he said.

"A week or two?" I asked.

"Yes Graham, it's important to make sure that you have control over yourself over a period of time," he said.

I nodded.

I went back to the window to take my medicine and then went in my room and lay down to take a nap.

2 weeks later

"Take care of yourself Graham. The best gift you could give us is that we never see you again," the head nurse said as she gave me a hug.

"I will, thank you," I said as I packed my duffle bag, and they walked me outside.

When I got outside, I saw the van there and everyone came out to greet me. I just walked into the center of them all and got a giant group hug. I started to cry. The emotion of the moment was completely overwhelming.

"How do you feel Graham?" Jackson asked.

"I feel great. I feel better than I have in a long time," I said.

Hannah clapped her hands over her face and started to cry. I walked up to her and gave her a giant kiss.

"Come on, let's get you home," Jean said as he patted my shoulder.

"We need to stop off at CVS so I can get my medicine first," I said.

"Of course!" Rosette said as she looked at me and smiled.

We went to CVS, and I got my medicine. We made our way back to our house.

"What are we supposed to do now that our house is paid off 30 years before it should be paid off?" Hannah asked.

"Just live our lives," I said.

We pulled up to the house and went inside, careful to disable the trip wire when we went in. We went upstairs and froze. There was a man in our living room smoking cigarettes.

"Look buddy, I don't know who you are, but you're in the wrong house," I said.

He looked at me and nodded.

"This isn't a joke buddy, don't make me remove you," Jackson said.

"Don't bother Jackson, I won't be long," the man said.

"How do you know my name?" Jackson asked.

The man took a deep drag off his cigarette and put it in the plastic cup full of water on the table.

"We have a serious problem, and we need your help," the man said turning to me.

"No man. I'm fresh out of rehab and I'm feeling good. I'm not getting involved in this kind of thing again. This is what set me off in the first place," I said.

"Graham, please. There's nobody else that can help us out on this," the man said.

"What's going on up here?" Josh asked.

"Ah, Josh. Good to see you. You'll be great help this time," the man said.

"What the actual hell are you talking about?" I asked.

"There is a very deep society that has done something truly terrible and we need your help to fix it. Nice beard Graham. You're barely recognizable. That will help you."

"What did you mean I'll be great help?" Josh asked.

The man lit another cigarette, took a drag and filled our living room up with smoke. Hannah turned the ceiling fan on.

"For your intricate knowledge of the occult and satanism," the man said.

"What do you want?" I asked.

"Supposedly there is a massive bomb hidden away someplace that will destroy our ability to sustain humanity. We need you to find it," the man said.

I thought about everything I had been through. I just wanted to live a normal life at this point. Upon further consideration I was willing to die for my beliefs and we have created so much good in the world. If I could help, I was going to try, knowing everything that comes with it.

"I don't suppose you have a clue for us or any pertinent information regarding this?" Rosette asked.

The man took a deep drag. "It's not a clue, it's a who," he said.

"Who then would that be?" I asked.

The man looked us over one by one and dropped his cigarette in the water cup.

"The Pindar," he said.

Coming Soon!

Into the Rabbit Hole
The Final Type
By Micah T. Dank

The Final Type, Book Six, the continuation of *Into the Rabbit Hole*: After discovering the Library of Alexandria Graham internalized all the wisdom from the books. This is crucial because the Pindar is still out there and the people she has tied herself to have planted 2 Coke can sized nuclear bombs inside what might be our last effort at saving humanity should a cataclysm hit. It's off to the races to discover where they are because the consequences would devastate our planet for the rest of our existence.

For more information
visit: www.SpeakingVolumes.us

Coming Soon!

A Cotten Stone Mystery
The Grail Conspiracy
By Lynn Sholes and Joe Moore

"This page-turner is bound to show up on
Da Vinci Code read-alike lists at public
libraries across the country."—*Library Journal*

The Grail Conspiracy, Book One, of the *Cotten Stone* series:
On assignment in the Middle East, television journalist Cotten
Stone stumbles upon an archeological dig that uncovers the
world's most-sought-after religious relic: The Holy Grail.
With his last dying breath, Dr. Gabriel Archer gives it to
Cotten, uttering "You are the only one" in a language she's
heard from only one other person–her deceased twin sister…

For more information
visit: www.SpeakingVolumes.us

On Sale Now!

MICAH DANK'S
INTO THE RABBIT HOLE series

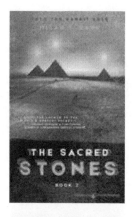

**For more information
visit:** www.SpeakingVolumes.us

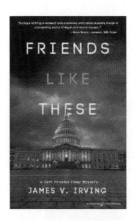

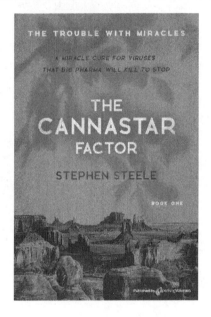

Sign up for free and bargain books

Join the Speaking Volumes mailing list

Text
ILOVEBOOKS
to 22828 to get started.

Message and data rates may apply.

Manufactured by Amazon.ca
Bolton, ON